"We've got him!"

Askart yelled. The captain remained silent, listening.

"What is the enemy's condition?"

The sonarman was silent for a moment, then switched the set to loudspeaker. The command center was suddenly filled with metallic groans, pops, and a grinding sound that made everyone's skin crawl.

"Breaking up, Captain," Askart observed. "You got him!"

The captain was silent, his expression unreadable.

Sixty men dead in that Russian, Patno thought to himself, over a hundred in the English boat. How many, he wondered, how many more of us will die underwater today?

DEEPCORE 2: BOOMER DOWN

This bo
the new
Swampl

Berkley Books by James B. Adair

THE *DEEPCORE* SERIES

DEEPCORE
DEEPCORE 2: BOOMER DOWN

THE *WORLD WAR III: BEHIND THE LINES* SERIES
(with Gordon Rottman)

TARGET TEXAS
TARGET NUKE
TARGET IRAN

DEEPCORE 2
BOOMER DOWN

JAMES B. ADAIR

B
BERKLEY BOOKS, NEW YORK

DEEPCORE 2: BOOMER DOWN

A Berkley Book / published by arrangement with the author

PRINTING HISTORY
Berkley edition / February 1992

ISBN: 0-425-13180-7

A BERKLEY BOOK ® TM 757,375
Berkley Books are published by The Berkley Publishing Group, 200 Madison Avenue, New York, New York 10016.

PRINTED IN THE UNITED STATES OF AMERICA

10 9 8 7 6 5 4 3 2 1

BOOMER DOWN

1

Bob Moore barely had the door open when the first flashbulb went off in his face.

"Arrhh!" he groaned, turning his face away with a grimace that was recorded by half a dozen other flashing cameras. The semicircle of reporters and photographers had waited patiently to ambush Moore and the other members of the UnderSea Security Department as they emerged from the Federal Building. Now the strobe lights fired a photon barrage at them, the motor-driven cameras blazing away like machine guns.

"Oh, shit," Carla Fuentes, coming out the door behind Moore, muttered under her breath. She whipped the Ray·Ban shades out of her jacket pocket and slipped them on as the whirring and flashing crescendoed.

Concentrating on Carla, the photographers almost missed Tyrone King and Tom Jackson who slipped out the door and walked quickly in the other direction. A few reporters pursued them for a few steps, then decided to stay with the leader and the glamour queen.

As King and Jackson made their escape, the mob hounded Moore and Fuentes all the way to their car.

"Mr. Moore," one cried, shoving a microphone in Bob's face, "is it true that the attackers were Russians?"

Moore shook his head. "We don't know who they were," he answered, pushing for the car door.

"Ms. Fuentes," another shouted at Carla, "were you physically assaulted?" Carla ignored the question. A woman reporter pushed past her colleagues.

"Were you raped?" she demanded. Carla turned and pulled down her shades to look at her interrogator. The woman, a spent piece of used television trash with an inch of makeup on her face and hair that looked like a fiberglass helmet, was holding her microphone in front of her like a rifle and bayonet.

"No," Carla spat.

"But we have heard reports," the harridan went on, her voice rising.

"Wait a minute!" Carla said loudly, smiling at the strident woman. "I know you! You had that really boring talk show!"

The reporter looked stricken and tried to press her question. The other reporters, amused at this unexpected twist, turned their mikes toward her.

"Ms. Fuentes," she stammered. Carla pressed her counterattack.

"Geez, Letterman creamed you!" she commiserated. "I really felt sorry for you!"

Unused to being on the receiving end of such attention, the woman melted back into the crowd amid laughter from her peers.

While Carla held the press at bay, Moore took the opportunity to get the car unlocked.

"Come on, Carla!" he shouted as he pulled the door open and slipped inside. She was right behind him, twisting into the seat as she slid the shades back on.

Moore ignored the press of bodies leaning on the car and tapping on the windows as he backed out of the parking space and pulled out of the parking lot into the heavy downtown traffic. Carla waved to the crowd of news hounds as they drove away.

"What a goddamn zoo!" Moore snapped as the knot of

reporters disappeared in the rearview mirror. "I thought after we spent days spilling our guts to Naval Intelligence, the fuckin' CIA, and the FBI, we'd get a little rest, but nooo."

"The curse of popularity, Bob," Carla observed. Despite her protests to the contrary, Moore could see that Carla liked the attention.

"If those nosy little shits find out those guys we killed on DeepCore were Spetsnaz," he speculated, "we'll be cursed for sure." He glanced over at her. "The feds'll stick us in jail so far back that they'll have to pipe in sunlight."

"They can't do anything to us," she retorted, "we were the good guys, remember?"

"To keep from getting in to it with the Russians," Moore answered, "they'd make our victim status permanent! I guarantee you that." A deeper tone crept into his voice. "I've been on enough spooky jobs before to know how these guys think. They could care less about us."

Moore glanced at his side mirror just in time to see a white minivan pull alongside. The van was emblazoned with the logo of a local TV station. In the backseat, a video cameraman had his lens trained on them.

"Oh, God," Moore moaned. He flicked on the turn indicator and pulled in front of the news van, nearly forcing it onto the median. In seconds, the minivan was lost in traffic behind them.

"Carla," Moore said emphatically, "we gotta get out of town or these bloodsuckers will never leave us alone." She nodded in agreement.

"When we get back to the office," he went on, "I'm asking the Old Man for some vacation time for all of us until this blows over."

"Good idea," Carla agreed. "I'd like to get out of town, way out of town." She suddenly pulled off her shades and turned sideways in the seat.

"You know where we could go!" she blurted. "Doesn't the company have a place down in Belize? Some kind of resort?"

"Yes, ma'am, it does"—Moore smiled—"and that's a damn good idea! Sun, fun, and quiet beaches sure sounds good to me. I'll ask him about it as soon as we hit the door."

"No way!" Marc LeFlore blurted. "No way are those fuckers going to come back here, hog all the glory, and then get a vacation trip to boot! No way!"

"I'm just telling you what Mr. Moore said when he called," Sheila, LeFlore's secretary, answered. "He said that he needed to get his people out of the spotlight. He was going to ask for some time off for them and for you to meet him upstairs in the boss's office at three-thirty." When LeFlore scowled, she added, "Don't kill me, I'm just the messenger."

"Sorry," LeFlore apologized, "I know it's not your fault, but this really pisses me off!" The sudden burst of emotion made the itch in his trousers flare to life. LeFlore turned for his own office, fighting the urge to scratch his private parts.

In his office, LeFlore shut the door and crossed to the wide windows behind his desk. Outside, a station wagon from one of the local TV stations sat parked across the street from UnderSea Corporation's main gate. A tall man in a safari jacket stood talking into a microphone as a cameraman filmed him, using the UnderSea Corporation building as the background.

LeFlore twisted the rod that closed the silver miniblinds and bent over, scratching his crotch with gusto, his eyes rolled up in pained ecstasy.

Goddamned hot tub! he silently cursed, slumping into his chair. The accident in his apartment complex's communal hot tub had scalded him from the waist down. Worse, half the complex had been there to witness it. It was one thing to have your nuts boiled, but having the whole world watch you do it was worse. Now the burn was peeling and it itched like fire. LeFlore pulled the blinds apart to watch the television crew outside.

A thousand cameras out there, he thought bitterly, and none of 'em will look at me! Fuck Bob Moore and his cretins!

LeFlore glanced at his gold Rolex. He had to be upstairs in five minutes. There was no time to scotch Moore's plan before he saw McLaughlin.

"Just wait, Bobby baby," LeFlore muttered, scratching vigorously, "just you wait!"

"Sir," Moore began, "my people are being hounded by the press so bad that we can't get anything done!" The Old Man leaned back in his chair, his fingers tented on his chest.

"Besides," Moore went on, "I'm afraid that our little secret will get out and there will be hell to pay with the government." McLaughlin nodded, his eyes closed. It seemed that the CEO was almost asleep.

"What I propose," Moore continued, "is that my people get their two weeks vacation now so they can hide out until the heat's off."

"And what is the company supposed to do for a security department for two weeks?" LeFlore interrupted.

"Same as it's doing right now," Moore answered. "The way the media are on us, we can't take a piss without *60 Minutes* being there to film it!"

LeFlore bristled. "You can't expect the company to—"

"Relax, Marc," McLaughlin said softly, sitting up and resting his elbows on the polished desk. "Bob and his people have saved the company literally millions of dollars, not to mention the lives of dozens of people."

"Well, I know that," LeFlore stammered, "but that is no reason for his people to—"

"On the contrary," McLaughlin interrupted, "I think it's a perfect reason." He looked at Moore and smiled.

"Bob, tell your troops that they can go on vacation for two weeks. We'll pick up the tab." McLaughlin's eyes twinkled knowingly. "Within reason."

"Thank you, sir," Moore answered, turning to LeFlore. "Marc, what's the status of that place in Belize the company bought last year?"

LeFlore looked puzzled for a second, then brightened suspiciously. "It's still in renovation," he answered, "why?"

"I'd like to go there," Moore replied. "Do a little scuba diving, get some sun for a change."

"Well, I don't know," LeFlore quibbled, "it's still not finished."

McLaughlin cut him off. "That sounds like a great place, Bob," he agreed.

Moore nodded. "Definitely."

"Have a good time then," McLaughlin said, rising from his chair. Moore and LeFlore stood, too. "Marc, see that Bob gets whatever he needs," he instructed LeFlore, then looked back at Moore.

"Don't worry about the press, Bob," he assured Moore. "By the time you get back, something else will have happened to someone else and they won't even remember your name."

"I hope so, sir," Moore answered. McLaughlin held out his hand and Moore shook it. "Thanks again." McLaughlin waved away his thanks.

"This company owes you, Bob," he argued, "all of you."

Moore smiled again, turned and left the room. LeFlore stayed behind to protest the plan.

"Sir, I don't think that the company should encourage this

kind of behavior," he complained. "I know that the Security Department did a good job on DeepCore, but that is what we pay them for!"

"We don't pay them enough for what they did, Marc," McLaughlin answered. "We're getting off cheap, believe me!"

LeFlore started to answer, but the Old Man's look cut him off. LeFlore nodded and started for the door. "I'll make sure they get whatever they need," he assured McLaughlin, who was not listening. He was already on the phone to the Public Relations Department, dictating a statement for release to the press.

The land below was a dark, emerald-green sea of jungle virtually unbroken by signs of civilization. The TACA Airlines 737's shadow raced along, dipping and leaping beneath them. Carla finished her immigration form and craned her head to see better out the round window.

"Bob," she asked, "are you sure this is near the capital city? I don't see anything!"

"Trust me," he answered, "Belize City is in front of us. That's why you can't see it."

"Must not be very big," Carla observed as the stewardess came on the intercom and told the passengers to buckle up and stow their tray tables. A few minutes later the runway flashed under them, lined on both sides by huge camouflage nets and sinister Rapier antiaircraft missile launchers. The plane came to a stop in front of a tiny, weathered building.

"Is that the terminal?" she asked. Moore nodded. She rolled her eyes.

"The new one isn't finished yet," he explained, pointing out the windows on the other side of the plane. Carla bent over to look at the large, half-finished modern building at the far end of the tarmac.

"Speed is not a great priority down here," Moore remarked.

"That's okay," she answered, "I keep forgetting that we're down here to unwind and hide out."

"I understand," he agreed, "it takes getting used to!"

The trip through passport control and customs was uneventful, although the passport inspector seemed quite curious about the large number of stamps from around the world in both their passports.

The taxi ride from the international airport to the smaller municipal airport was far more harrowing than the flight. When the ancient Pontiac station wagon lurched to a halt, both passengers looked relieved. Moore paid the driver, who disappeared in a cloud of blue-gray smoke.

"Are we relaxing yet?" Carla asked hopefully.

"Soon," Moore answered. "The flight to the island will only take an hour."

She scanned the collection of small private planes parked in the sun next to the tiny terminal. "Which one of these beauties are we on?"

"None of these," Moore answered. "Here comes ours, now." He pointed to a dark speck low in the sky off the far end of the runway. As they watched, the speck turned into an ungainly airplane that seemed to hang in the sky. A few moments later the plane dropped onto the short runway. The engines, barely audible a moment before, roared as the pilot reversed the propellors, slowing the plane even more.

"Twin Otter," Moore explained, "lands and takes off on a dime."

"I hope we've got plenty of change, then," Carla observed as the plane came to a stop next to the terminal.

With no formality and little that passed for organization, the plane's two-man crew picked up their bags, loaded them into the small cargo bay, and herded them on board.

When everyone was seated, the plane rolled forward and suddenly jumped into the heavy air.

An hour later the landing on East Point Island made the takeoff seem boring. The island's landing strip was shorter than a football field and perilously narrow. The Twin Otter seemed to fall onto the concrete and stick there, then backed up to the concrete pad in front of a galvanized Quonset hut.

"Well," Carla said with a laugh, following Bob Moore down the stairs, "that was exciting!"

"Mr. Moore?" a blond, deeply tanned young man asked, looking at a small list in his hand.

"Right," Moore replied, "and this is Carla Fuentes."

"Great!" the blond said. "I'm Greg Master. I'll get your bags." He gathered the dive bags and loaded them into a waiting golf cart. When they were loaded, the Otter's crew waved good-bye and climbed back aboard. The plane backed up to the end of the runway, revved its two turboprop engines, rolled forward, and leaped up into the sky.

"Welcome to East Point," Master said as the two new visitors climbed into the cart. Master switched the cart on and drove the hundred yards to the cluster of concrete cabins just off the beach.

As he pulled up in front of the first cabin, Master went into his tour guide speech.

"All our cabins are air-conditioned," he began, pulling Carla's luggage out of the golf cart, "although you probably won't need it. The breeze here is cool at night." He set her bags up on the concrete porch and then walked up the three steps to open the door. Moore and Carla followed.

Inside, the room was simple but comfortable. There was a mahogany double bed, a desk, two mahogany lawn chairs, and a mahogany bedside table.

"You can snorkel right off the beach," Master continued,

"but if you want to scuba, please let one of us know so we can divemaster you."

Carla greeted this warning with a skeptical glance.

"Bob and I are both divemasters," she interrupted. "We do this for a living, too."

"Oh, yeah," Master apologized, setting down the bags, "I forgot you folks are from the company. I've been practicing this speech over and over for when we open to the public."

"We understand," Moore said. He gave Carla a look that said "lighten up."

"Anyway," Master went on, walking back out to the golf cart, "filled tanks are in the Quonset hut at the end of the dock." He reached for Moore's bags and started back up the stairs. Moore stopped him and pointed to the next cabin.

"I'm next door, Greg," Moore reminded him. Master looked confused for a second, then smiled sheepishly and started for the next cabin.

"Sorry," he mumbled as he disappeared up the steps into Moore's cabin.

"Thanks, Greg," Moore said when the young man emerged, "we'll want to go out first thing in the morning."

Master seemed to be looking at Carla in a different way now.

"Great!" he said, slipping behind the wheel. "Around here, first thing starts about nine."

"Perfect," Carla answered. Master waved and drove away, leaving the two newcomers alone. They stood looking at the swaying palms and the turquoise water that stretched to the horizon.

"This is like heaven," Carla observed.

"I'll say one thing," Moore replied, looking at the cabins, "I've stayed in uglier safe houses." Carla laughed. They stood silently looking at the tropical paradise for another minute.

"Well," Moore said finally, "I think I'm going to bag

it. I don't think I've had a decent sleep since we left for DeepCore." He left Carla leaning on the rail around her front porch, staring at the beach and the waves.

In his cabin, he flopped back on the bed, letting the tension of the last few weeks flow out of him. In less than a minute, Bob Moore was sound asleep.

"Tell me again how much fun this is," Tyrone King gasped as he hooked his toes over the tiny nubbin of rock and heaved himself up.

"Stop whining," Tom Jackson admonished, pulling the slack out of the thick nylon climbing rope, "you said you wanted to get away from all the attention." Jackson leaned forward and looked down the sheer rock face below them. "No way anyone'll find us here."

"No one'll find our dead bodies if we fall off this mother, either," King argued. Jackson was six feet above him on the ledge, braced against the rocks to catch King if he slipped during his ascent.

King surveyed the wall above him. There were a few spots that might hold his weight. He reached above and to the right, jamming his fingers into a thin crack as he put his weight against another small nubbin of granite and pulled himself up two more feet.

His hand felt like it was in a vise. He quickly found a small indentation in the rock and curled the fingers on his left hand into it. His right hand came out of the crack bleeding from the scratches over his knuckles.

"Come on," Jackson urged, "this is the easy part!"

"Don't tell me that, man," King snapped, "I don't want to know if the rest of it's worse."

King studied the rock face and plotted his next two moves. He reached up with his right hand, jamming it into the crack higher up.

"Okay," he warned Jackson, "here I come!"

In two quick moves, he was up to the ledge.

"See," Jackson scolded him, "that wasn't so hard."

"Yo mama," King observed, pulling his small daypack off his back to get at the canteen inside. He tipped the plastic bottle up and poured the cold Gatorade down his parched throat.

"Oh, shit!" Jackson blurted.

"What?" King asked, looking hesitantly over the edge. Three hundred feet below them, a television news van had pulled up beside their tent. They watched in disappointment as a woman in slacks and a safari jacket stepped from the van, microphone in hand. Behind her came the cameraman, tilting his lens up to the ledge where they sat.

"So much for getting away," King complained, looking over at his partner's irritated face. Jackson stood.

"Only one thing to do now, I guess," Jackson said. King waited for the punch line.

"We'll loop the climbing rope around our necks and throw ourselves off," he explained. "Our suicide will protest our harassment by the media!"

The two men looked at each other for a long second.

"Naaaaaa!" They both laughed in unison, turning to put more of the wall between themselves and their electronic pursuers.

The sun was an orange ball on the horizon when Carla wandered into the small restaurant. It looked closed, but there was one table set next to the center window, waiting for the only two guests in the resort. Behind the carved dark wood bar, Greg Master was polishing a tall glass.

"I wondered if you would be in tonight," he said as Carla stepped up to the bar and eased her tight white shorts into the tall chair.

"Are you the bartender, too?" she asked.

"Chief cook and bar back," he said, holding up the shining glass, "I do a lot of different chores around here. Sort of a jack-of-all-trades."

"Well, Jack," she said, "how about a margarita?"

"Coming up," Master replied. He salted the rim of a tulip glass, filled a shaker with tequila, triple sec, and fresh lime juice, tossed in a handful of shaved ice, shook it briskly, poured it in the tulip glass, and set it down in front of her. She knocked back a large gulp, smiling at him over the rim of the glass. As the liquor hit, she whistled.

"You make a mean margarita!" she observed.

"Down here," he explained, "it costs less to use the real stuff than to import all that phony drink mix. Everything you get here is straight."

"I'll bet that's right," she said, looking him over from head to foot. He tried to ignore her appraisal and quickly changed the subject.

"So, are you two just here on a vacation," he asked, "or on company business?"

"A little of both," she answered. "We needed to get away for a while. This seemed like a good place to hide out."

"The best," he agreed. "No one comes out here. The tour boats don't come out this far and it costs too much to get here by charter boat." He looked up as the sun slid beneath the waves, lighting the sky a vivid orange. "Once every blue moon, we get a government patrol boat out here, but they usually don't get this far from land. We're pretty isolated."

"So what brought you out here?" Carla asked, stirring the drink with her straw.

Master's eyes seemed to focus out past the horizon, an odd, faraway look on his face.

"I got tired of the world," he answered, his eyes shifting

back to hers. "I just got tired of being the slowest rat in the race. You know what I mean?"

"Yeah, I think so"—she nodded—"I've been there, too." She downed the last of the margarita in a long gulp. Master's eyes grew big as the potent drink disappeared between her dark red lips.

"So, what's for dinner?" she asked, licking away the last bits of white foam.

"Aren't you going to wait for your friend?" he asked. She smiled.

"He's my boss," she explained. "He's been so stressed, he may sleep for days!"

Master nodded. "Well, dinner tonight is red snapper filet on rice with a lime sauce from Louisiana and a local bean dish I think you'll like." He raised his eyebrows. "Are you ready for it now?"

"I'm always ready for it," she answered, fixing him with a look that made him blush.

"I'll get right on it," he stammered, "I mean it'll just take a minute." He flushed again. "I mean," he said slowly, "I will go fix your dinner right now."

"I can hardly wait." She smiled as he backed nervously into the kitchen.

As she waited for her dinner, Carla watched the day's last dying lights turn the sky from orange to mauve to a thin blue-purple line under the bright mantle of stars.

She shook her head. It seemed like a year since the attack on DeepCore, not just a few weeks. Already, the memory had taken on a surreal quality like some vivid dream in which she had fought and killed the strangers in black uniforms in metal corridors deep under the Pacific.

The sea outside these windows was a gentle sea whose slow waves broke in pale green phosphorescent crests around the restaurant's short pier, beckoning her.

A wonderful aroma broke into her reverie and she turned as Master set the large plate of steaming fish in front of her.

"Snapper à la East Point," he said brightly as she smiled up at him. "I took the liberty of bringing myself a plate. May I?"

"Of course," she answered. Master slid into the chair next to her and poured them both a glass of pale white wine. He raised his glass.

"To new friends," he toasted. Their glasses rang like bells as they touched.

The moon was up an hour later when he walked her to her cabin.

"How about a nightcap?" she asked. He frowned.

"You really shouldn't have any more alcohol if you're going to dive tomorrow."

Carla smiled and took his hand. "I've got a Diet Coke in my luggage."

"That would be good," he answered as she led him up the concrete steps to her room.

"Sidney, I'm really bored!" Melinda whined. "You promised me this cruise would be fun!"

Sidney Grunwald ran his short, stubby fingers through his thinning hair, looking for the patience to soothe his increasingly irritating client.

Ten platinum albums and two hit movies had not changed Melinda Pettering. She was a bitch and always had been.

Grunwald had booked this trip to get her out of Hollywood for a while. He was afraid she was working too hard and about to burn out. She was also up to three grams a day of Peruvian marching powder and Sidney had seen the results of that habit before.

He had sold Melinda on the cruise by arranging to have a *Playboy* photo shoot in Jamaica when they finally docked there. They'd boarded the sailing yacht *Obsession,* a sleek ninety-foot motorsailer, in Monterey, Mexico. The plan was to sail down to Roatán and then over to Jamaica.

The Mexican press had swarmed all over them and Grunwald had been afraid they would never get out of port for the boatloads of photographers that had choked the harbor, trying to get a shot of La Melinda.

Melinda herself had, of course, loved the hysterical attention. The adoration of her fans kept her pumped up more than the most potent Peruvian flake.

Now, three days out, she was bored and petulant. Her latest stud, Lars, a bodybuilder from Venice Beach, was seasick and unable to provide her with the usual Herculean hosing. It promised to be a long crossing to Jamaica.

Oh, well, Sidney mused, maybe I'll write up the trip, sell it as a film package, and clean up that way. That thought cheered him.

Eager to escape Melinda's whining, Sidney went down to the salon for a drink. He was pouring a tall gin and tonic when the *Obsession*'s captain stepped out of his small aft cabin.

Ben Danforth looked like a sea captain from central casting. He was tall and thin, his face dark from the tropical sun. His steel-gray eyes never betrayed a moment's doubt or hesitation. Best of all, he was totally unimpressed with his passengers' fame or wealth.

"Care for a cocktail, Captain?" Sidney asked, holding up the emerald-green bottle of Tanqueray.

"Thanks, no," Danforth answered. Sidney shrugged and went back to pouring.

"So how're we doing?" Sidney went on, hoping to engage the captain in conversation to avoid going back up on deck.

"We're doing well, Mr. Grunwald," Danforth answered. "We should make Roatán by late tomorrow night."

"Great!" Sidney gushed. "That's great." Danforth stood looking at him. For some reason, being stared at by those gray eyes always made him nervous. Sometimes they looked like two ball bearings.

"Gosh," Sidney stammered, "the sea really looks big at night. It kinda makes you feel like you're the only one in the whole world."

"Indeed," Danforth answered, "but it's deceptive sometimes. We have a friend out here with us now." Danforth motioned for Grunwald to follow him to the tiny navigation station in the corridor leading to Danforth's cabin.

In the center of the navigation panel, the radar set's green circle glowed brightly. Danforth pointed to a white dot at the bottom of the screen.

"She's been there since we left Monterey," he explained. "Sometimes she disappears off the scope, but she always comes back."

Grunwald looked at the white dot, then up at the captain.

"Are they following us?"

"Maybe"—Danforth shrugged—"maybe just going to the same place."

"What are you going to do?" Grunwald asked, suddenly concerned.

"Nothing," Danforth answered. "No law against following somebody." He looked at Grunwald's pinched expression and smiled.

"Relax, Mr. Grunwald," he reassured the anxious mariner, "if they get any closer, we'll hail them." This didn't seem to have any effect on Grunwald. "Besides," Danforth went on, "we're not exactly babes at sea on this boat. We can take care of ourselves."

That news seemed to make Grunwald even more apprehensive. Danforth patted him on the shoulder and went up the stairs to the wheelhouse, leaving Grunwald below, gulping his gin.

The morning dawned clear and calm. Master was gone when Carla woke up. She slipped out of bed, wrapped the thin robe around her, and stepped out onto the porch.

Master and Bob Moore were at the end of the dock. Moore had his hands jammed into his pockets, his shoulders rolled forward. Master was pointing at something off to the right.

The sea looked like glass, perfect for diving. Bob Moore turned and saw her. He waved and cupped his hands to shout at her.

"Come on!" he yelled. "We're ready when you are!"

She nodded and waved, then turned back into her room. She was tying the knot on her bikini top when Moore knocked.

"Want some coffee?" he called through the door.

"Yeah!" she yelled back. "Come on in!" Moore came through the door with a pair of yellow UnderSea Corporation coffee cups in his hands and an aluminum thermos under his arm.

"Great, Bob, thanks," Carla said, bending down to pull the turquoise stretch Lycra dive suit out of her bag.

Moore was trying not to stare at her breasts, which threatened to jump ship from her skimpy red bikini top at any moment. He poured two cups of coffee and stood looking out the open door as she slithered into the skintight suit.

"We couldn't have a better day," he remarked as she pulled the zipper up to her cleavage and took a sip from the steaming coffee.

"When's the last time you went diving just for fun?" she asked, perching on the edge of the rumpled bed.

He looked at her with a puzzled expression. "I honestly can't remember," he admitted, "I don't think it was in this decade."

"Come on, then," she said, laughing. She stood up on tiptoes and kissed Moore on the cheek.

"What was that for?" he asked, his expression even more puzzled.

"For hiring me"—she laughed—"and for bringing me here." She drained the coffee and shouldered her mesh dive bag. "Let's go!"

The boat ride to East Point Reef was short. The morning air and the salt spray were invigorating. Master, looking a bit tired, was all business. Carla played along, but from Bob Moore's bemused looks, she doubted that their encounter was any secret.

More likely, everybody on the island knew about it this morning. Cecil Estevan, the resort's chief caretaker and boat driver, was smiling like a Cheshire cat as he deftly steered them out to the reef.

Her Seiko dive watch read 9:55 when Carla set the bezel and stepped off the side of the boat.

East Point Reef was forty-five feet below the surface. Ten miles long, it was almost virgin coral. The water was clear as gin.

The three of them took their time, lazily meandering along the reef wall, letting the slow current do most of the work for them.

The reef was home to thousands of tropical fish as well as countless eels, sea turtles, and other reef dwellers. They slowly kicked their way along, blissed out in the beautiful fantasy world.

At one point, Master yodeled at them and pointed farther down the reef. A sea turtle the size of a Volkswagen swam beneath them, its big flippers sweeping back and forth like oars.

Carla was surprised when Master swam up and held his pressure gauge up, pointing at it. She pulled her own gauge up. Eight hundred pounds remained in her tank.

That has to be wrong, she thought, looking at her watch. It was 10:45. They had been down fifty minutes that seemed like fifty seconds.

Master pointed up, signaling the end of the dive. The three divers slowly kicked their way to the surface and inflated their buoyancy compensators to keep them afloat until the dive boat motored over to pick them up. The wind had picked up a bit and the surface waves were a foot high. Cecil helped each diver get their equipment in the boat.

They were pulling up to the dock when Ramon, Cecil's brother and East Point's only other full-time employee, came running out of the office, frantically waving a piece of yellow paper.

By the time they stopped, Ramon was there, his eyes wide with excitement and fear.

"Mr. Greg!" he shouted at Master. "Mayday, Mayday!" Master stepped off the boat as it bumped against the dock and took the piece of paper Ramon had been waving. He read it quickly, then turned to Bob Moore and read it aloud.

"Mayday, *Obsession* under attack by armed pirates," he read. "Need immediate assistance and medical evacuation." Master looked up, amazed at the message.

Moore jumped to the dock and took the paper, then turned to Ramon.

"When did you receive this?"

"Just now!" Ramon blurted. "On the emergency channel." He pointed at the office.

Moore turned to Master. "Where are these coordinates?"

"About sixty miles east of here," Master answered as Carla stepped onto the dock next to them.

"I hope somebody can get to them in time," she said.

"There really isn't anybody to get there," Master replied. "The government only has four patrol craft and they're not allowed outside the twelve-mile limit."

"What about the Brits?" Moore asked. "Don't they have choppers here?"

"Not on the coast," Master explained, "they're all inland, looking for smugglers from Guatemala."

"Then I guess we'll have to help them ourselves," Moore observed. "You got any guns here?"

"A shotgun, a rifle," Master answered, "and a very illegal 9mm pistol."

"Get 'em!"

Moore turned to Cecil, who was staring openmouthed at them. "Can this boat make it out sixty miles and back?" Cecil's look turned from amazement to injured pride.

"Of course," he answered, "this is a good boat!"

"I hope so," Moore called over his shoulder as he ran up the dock after Master.

"He's dead!" Melinda shrieked. "They're all dead!"

Danforth shouldered his way past her to the wrecked navigation station. The panel above the desk was shattered and smoking, the radar, radio, and satellite navigation gear wrecked beyond repair. The single rocket had hit where it would do the most damage without sinking the yacht.

The pirates had attacked during breakfast. The three passengers had been eating in the main salon. As usual, Melinda had been whining about the food, her blond stud pup had been sick, and her manager had looked like the before picture in a Tums ad.

The alarm on the radar had gone off when the boat was ten miles away. It took less than fifteen minutes for the powerful cigarette boat to close the distance.

They had raked *Obsession* with machine-gun fire on the first pass, killing Wally at the helm and wounding Danforth. Patsy, the cook, had gotten off a Mayday message before the pirates came around again and hit them with the rocket, stopping all communication and ripping poor Patsy apart.

Melinda's stud, Lars, acting on some heroic impulse, ran out on deck and was shot down like a big dog. Danforth and Bobby Rollins, the steward, had fought back with the sailboat's only weapons, a shotgun and the flare pistol. One of the flares had started a fire on the pirate boat and it had run away, trailing smoke. Bobby had been killed by a final burst from the sorry bastards.

Now they were adrift. Danforth had been hit in the chest, high up on the right side. The wound ached, but there were no bubbles coming from it. That was the good news. The bad news was that he could hardly fire the shotgun if the pirates came back, much less sail the boat.

Melinda was a basket case and her manager was no help. She had fled to the forward cabin, screaming. Grunwald was paralyzed by fear, rolled into a fetal position under the settee table.

"Well, Captain Ben," Danforth said to himself, "this time I think you've screwed the pooch!"

He made his way to the bar, poured two fingers of Chevas into a glass, and tossed back half of it. The Scotch burned its way down, taking the edge off the ache in his side. He counted the remaining shells in his pocket. Ten rounds of double-0 buckshot. Not much with which to repel boarders.

Danforth knocked back the rest of the Scotch, then pulled himself back up the stairs to the bloodstained cockpit. He would make his last stand from there.

"*Obsession,* this is East Point Resort," Master said into the microphone, "*Obsession,* do you read?" Only static answered. Master looked back at Moore and Carla, who were standing behind him.

"Nothing," he reported.

"Let's go take a look," Moore ordered, starting for the door. He picked up the shotgun and the pistol on the way out. Carla grabbed the rifle and Master followed them both, ordering Ramon to radio for help from anyone who could hear.

Cecil had the engine running as the three jumped aboard. He revved the big outboard and pulled the boat back from the dock, then gunned it for the open sea.

"How long will it take us to get there?" Carla asked.

"About three hours," Master answered.

"I hope they can hold off that long," she said, opening the box of rifle shells and slipping five rounds into the magazine.

"Oh, shit," she complained.

"What's the matter?" Master asked.

"I forgot that this dive suit doesn't have any pockets."

He laughed. "Indeed."

"Never mind," she answered, unzipping the dive suit down to her bikini top, "I used to carry a .357 snub-nose in here. I guess there's room for some .308s!"

"Um, yeah, probably," Master stammered as Carla laughed at his embarrassment.

Pablo Escobar winced as Jorje wrapped the gauze around his burnt forearm.

"Easy, *chinga madre!*" he cursed. "You're pulling off my skin!" Jorje shot him a look that said "then do it yourself." The burn didn't hurt Pablo as bad as the humiliation. The yacht crew had fought back skillfully. Most crews just caved in after the first burst of gunfire. Pablo and his crew had taken half a dozen boats in the last four years and none of them had fought back like this one.

Pablo had killed the man with the flare gun, but not before the *cholo* had managed to bounce a flare off him. The burning flare had rolled off his arm into the cabin and set fire to the upholstery there. It was a miracle that it had not spread to the fuel.

The fire was out now, but the cabin was still smoking, the fumes putrid smelling.

Those fuckers will pay for this, he promised. There couldn't be but one or two crew still alive on the boat. He had killed one himself and seen Jorje shoot the big blond man down on the deck. There had been another shooter on deck, too. Pablo thought he had hit the man, but he had disappeared below as the fire had broken out and Pablo had broken off the fight before they could finish him.

"I'll finish you in a few minutes, *pendejo,*" Pablo muttered. "I'll take my time, too. Maybe I'll fuck the movie star *puta* and let you watch." Cheered by that thought, Pablo set about fixing his boat for the next attack on the gringo's yacht.

"There it is!" Master shouted, pointing to a speck on the horizon just off the starboard bow.

"What does she look like?" Moore asked as Master focused the 10X50 Steiner binoculars on the stricken boat.

"She's got sails up, but I don't think anyone is at the helm," Master reported, passing the glasses to Moore.

"Somebody's sailing her," Moore answered, "or she'd be sailing a circle." He turned to Carla. "Get on the radio and see if you can raise them."

She picked up the radio mike and began to hail the beleaguered yacht. Moore brought the binoculars up again.

"There's a black spot on the hull," he observed, "and it looks like there's a body on the foredeck."

"Jesus," Master whispered.

Danforth's head snapped up, his neck popping from the sudden motion.

"Oww," he moaned, rubbing his neck with his still functioning left hand. Exhausted from the fight and weak from his wound, he had dozed off in the cockpit. He checked the compass. It was twenty degrees off, not as far as he'd feared.

His side ached and his right arm was stiffer now than before. The shotgun lay beneath his feet. If the pirates came back, he'd have to tie the wheel to use the gun.

He flipped up the cover over the engine controls and pressed the starter. The 100hp Westerbeke engine whined, but would not catch. One of the stray rounds from the gun battle had disabled it.

Danforth chuckled ruefully. He had begged the owners to armor the engine compartment, fuel tank, cockpit, and aft cabin when the big sloop had gone in for refit last summer, but the owners, a group of Chicago dentists, had patiently explained to him that the *Obsession* was a charter yacht, not a ninety-foot sail-powered PT boat.

"I wish you tooth fairies were here to explain that to me now," he muttered, switching off the useless engine. A cough racked his chest and Danforth bent double from the pain. He looked up to see Melinda's terrified face in the companionway hatch.

"Are we safe?" she demanded. Danforth forced a smile.

"I don't know," he answered. She screwed her face into an ugly scowl.

"Whaddaya mean you don't know?" she snarled. "You're the captain! Who else would know?" Danforth realized that he had never heard her grating New York accent before.

"I don't know if anyone heard our distress call," he explained, "I don't know if the assholes who jumped us are coming back, and I don't know for sure where we are."

"Well, what do you know?" she snarled as she stepped up into the cockpit. She had a bottle of vodka with her and plopped down on one of the long cushions and took a deep swig.

"I know that the boat's shot up," he answered, "I'm in bad shape, and you're from the Bronx."

She almost smiled at that, but something on the water caught her attention.

"They're back!" she screamed, flying down the stairs into the cabin and leaving Danforth alone with the vodka bottle that now spun wildly on the grating, sloshing its contents in every direction. A powerboat was coming in from the west.

Danforth picked up the bottle, took a deep swig, then threw the bottle over the side. He used his knee to brace the wheel as he picked up the shotgun and laid it next to him.

"Come and get it, motherfuckers," he barked, hoping the rough talk would scare away the fear rising inside him.

"I thought I saw someone in the cockpit," Master insisted as the yacht drew nearer. "Holy shit, there's a bunch of holes in her, all down the side."

"What about that guy on the deck?" Carla asked. "Is he alive?"

"He isn't moving," Master answered.

"Cecil," Moore said, "bring us alongside her from behind. We'll board her and see what we can do."

Cecil leaned on the wheel and slipped into the sailboat's wake. Across the stern was the name *Obsession.*

They were fifty yards from the yacht when a head popped up over the rim of the cockpit and a shot boomed across the water. The dive boat's windshield shattered, spraying tiny safety glass cubes.

Bob Moore scuttled over to the console and grabbed the small megaphone.

"*Obsession*," he bellowed through the bullhorn, "cease

fire! We are from East Point Resort! We're here to help you!" His only answer was silence.

"Hokay, this time, no more Señor Nice Guy!" Pablo insisted, rallying his troops for their final assault on the yacht. "We go straight in, we jump on the boat, and we shoot the fuck out of anybody that moves! You got it?"

The others, Jorje, Julio, and Leo, nodded their assent. Pablo could see the fear in their eyes. The other times had been easy, this one was not.

What chickenshits, Pablo thought as Leo pushed the throttles forward and the boat stepped up onto the water, its wake fanning out behind. These *pachucos* have had it too easy! They're too scared to sell drugs and too lazy to smuggle wetbacks. They've made a bundle ripping off these fancy boats and now they act scared. Shit!

They had made a fortune stealing boats. The man from Panama never asked questions and never seemed upset about a few holes in the sides. Pablo was careful to wash off any bloodstains.

They kept everything inside the boats. The Panamanian wanted them stripped of anything that could tie the boat to its previous, deceased owners. They had Bose stereos in their cars and Nikon cameras galore, not to mention the jewelry, watches, and cash.

Now and then, they picked up a playmate who was still alive, but they never seemed to last too long.

"Straight in and waste 'em!" Pablo reminded his crew. "Nothing fancy!" There would be no repetition of this morning's embarrassment!

"Thank you!" Melinda cried. "Oh, God, thank you, thank you, thank you!"

She was shaking and sobbing uncontrollably. Her makeup

still smeared down her face, her thick black hair a tangle.

"We knew we were dead!" her manager, a short, balding, little guy with a big belly and very little hair, jabbered. "They killed everyone else! They would have killed us, too, if you hadn't come!"

No one was really listening to him, but he went on and on about how unbelievable it all was and how he couldn't believe the crew was really dead and how wonderful they were to save them.

Carla and Danforth were on the plush circular settee where Carla had the yacht's first-aid kit out, treating his wound as Danforth told his story.

Bob Moore stood looking out the large porthole, sweeping the horizon with his binoculars. Master was below in the engine room, looking for the damage there.

"They'll be back," Danforth gasped as Carla pulled the dressing tight around his chest. "They took a hit, but they know they've got us. As soon as they get their shit together, they'll hit us again."

"Hopefully, we'll be gone before then," Moore assured Danforth. A throbbing shook the yacht as the diesel engine rumbled to life. Master's head appeared through the engine-room hatch.

"Got it fixed!" he announced. "The glow plugs weren't getting any juice. Wire was shot away. It'll run, now!"

"It'll have to," Moore answered, still staring through his binoculars, "we have company!"

"There it is, man"—Pablo laughed—"just where we left it!" He pounded on Leo's back. "Come on, faster! Let's take the motherfucker!"

Leo pushed the throttles forward an inch. The engines' whine increased a little. Pablo frowned and slammed the throttles forward. The engines roared and the cigarette boat lurched forward, slamming over the waves and pitching Julio and Jorje backward onto the bench seat.

"Now little *puta,*" Pablo shouted over the roaring engines and the pounding of the waves, "now you'll find out what fucking is."

"No way, Bob!" Master shouted.

"Greg," Moore answered, ushering the terrified rock star and her jellylike manager up the stairs, "I appreciate your concern and I'm not casting any aspersions on you at all. I need you to get these people to safety and protect them on the way." As Master followed him into the cockpit, Moore handed him Danforth's shotgun.

"Take this with you," he instructed Master, "I don't think they'll follow you, but take it anyway." Master took the gun, but was clearly unhappy about the order.

"Greg," Carla said softly, taking Master's arm, "this is what we do for a living. You take care of people and you're really good at it. These folks need you to take care of them."

She looked toward the east. The speedboat was much closer now, visible without the binoculars.

"We'll take care of these weasels," she assured the unhappy guide.

Cecil had pulled the dive boat alongside and now Melinda and Grunwald were scrambling aboard. Melinda looked like a rabbit caught in car headlights and her manager was a whimpering mass of cellulite.

"Go!" Moore urged Master, hooking his thumb toward the open sea. With a look of pained resignation, Master stepped aboard the dive boat. Cecil spun the small wheel and the boat sped away, keeping the yacht between itself and the pirate boat.

"I wish you had gone with them," Carla said to Danforth

as they stepped back down into the salon.

"You know I couldn't," Danforth gasped. "This expensive little toy is my responsibility. I can't get off until it docks. Or sinks."

"We understand," Moore answered. "Can you sail her?"

"I think so," Danforth said, struggling to his feet. Moore helped the wounded captain up and handed him the 9mm pistol.

"Just in case!" Moore said. Danforth took the pistol and forced out a smile.

"Here they come!" Carla called. The cigarette boat was closing the distance fast. Danforth struggled up the stairs and took the wheel. The engine throb increased as he pushed the diesel to full speed, turning the yacht away from the oncoming pirates.

"You ready?" Moore asked Carla as he stuffed another round into his nine-shot pump.

"No, but so what?" she answered.

"You go forward and use the hatch for cover," Moore suggested. "I'll go up with Danforth." She nodded and turned toward the forward stateroom.

Moore crawled up the stairs into the cockpit. Danforth was slumped down on the deck grating, steering the boat by compass heading. Moore peeked over the edge of the cockpit's teak rim. The pirates were less than two hundred yards away, steering to come up behind the yacht.

"Come left twenty degrees," Moore ordered Danforth. The yacht heeled as he spun the big wheel to port. Moore leaned down the stairs and called to Carla.

"Wait till they're close!" he shouted. "Fire on my shot."

Moore looked back over the rim. The boat had changed course and was now heading directly for the yacht. Moore looked down at Danforth, who looked very tired.

"Prepare to repel boarders!" Moore told him. Danforth

nodded and slipped the pistol out of the sling around his right arm.

The cigarette boat was coming alongside, its sleek, sharp nose sliding along the sailboat's hull. Moore gave Danforth a thumbs-up, took a deep breath, and whipped the shotgun up.

He fired at the powerboat's cockpit, shattering the windshield. On the foredeck, a short, dark man dropped the grapnel and coiled line he was holding and pulled a pistol from his belt.

A loud crack from the yacht's foredeck sent the man spinning over the far edge of the deck into the water. Carla was in action, too.

As Moore pumped another round into the shotgun, another pirate leaned around the shattered windshield and fired a burst from his MAC-10 submachine gun. A stream of 9mm slugs ripped through the teak.

Moore was already on the far side of the cockpit. He stuck the shotgun up over the rim and fired again as the two boats bumped. One of the pirates was screaming in Spanish. Moore pumped another round, fired over the railing at the sound, and dropped down into the cockpit as another burst ripped through the rim at the forward edge of the cockpit.

"Get inside!" he yelled at Danforth. The wounded captain was in no mood to argue. He released the wheel and slithered down the steps into the salon. Moore crawled backward to the steps, crouched, then stood up, the shotgun in front of him. There was a man on the afterdeck, trying to get to his feet after jumping over from the pirate boat. Moore blasted him with double-0 buck and jumped backward through the hatch as another fusillade ripped the polished wood overhead.

"Fuck!" Pablo cursed. They were fighting like demons again! He had not expected any fight at all, now half his men were dead.

Leo's face and neck were bleeding from a dozen cuts. The shot itself had missed him, but the glass had splattered him, slashing his pocked skin. Jorje had been shot right off the deck and now Julio lay bleeding on the yacht.

"Come on, man," Leo urged him, "let's go!"

"Fuck you!" Pablo screamed. "We are taking this fucking boat! You hear me?"

Leo's head snapped back as the bullet hit just above his right eye. The back of Leo's head seemed to explode, showering the white vinyl upholstery with specks of blood and bits of Leo's liquefied brains.

A sudden change of heart came over Pablo. He knocked Leo's body from the driver's seat and spun the wheel to the left until it locked. He pushed the throttles forward as far as they would go.

The cigarette boat lurched forward, heeling over as its propellors bit into the water.

Carla laid the cross hairs on the bloody face and fired. The recoil snapped her back and when she pulled the rifle down from her shoulder to pull the bolt back, the man was gone. As she shoved the bolt forward on a fresh round, the pirate boat roared to life and turned away from the yacht, headed away as fast as it could run.

She leaned up out of the hatch, wrapped the rifle sling around her left arm, and planted both elbows on the deck. Leaning into the rifle stock, she could see the pirate boat's driver through the scope.

The cigarette boat was slamming through the waves, her target pitching up and down in the scope. Carla shifted her aim to the sleek boat's stern and fired at a spot just above the water. She kept her face glued to the stock as she worked the bolt and fired again at the stern. There was one more round in the magazine. Carla aimed just above the water again and pulled the trigger.

A puff of white smoke coughed from the boat's exhaust. She fished around frantically in her bikini top for the extra rifle shells there, then jammed them into the magazine. More smoke was trailing from the pirate's exhaust and it seemed that the boat was slowing.

Carla slammed the bolt forward on a live round and brought the rifle up to her eye. She couldn't see the pirate himself, so she fired at the stern, worked the bolt and fired again.

She was pulling the bolt back for another shot when the pirate boat exploded. The fireball, orange with a fringe of black, was rising into the air like a miniature Hiroshima when the boom came rolling over the water.

"Nice shot," a voice said from below. Carla looked down at Bob Moore's upturned face.

"Lucky," she answered, raising the rifle over her head as she dropped down through the hatch. Moore caught her as she stumbled.

"You're lucky, too," she observed. "You could have gotten your ass shot off." He smiled and nodded in agreement.

"Come on, let's get our captain back to dry land," Moore suggested. "He needs it more than he's admitting."

Danforth had collapsed on the settee again. Carla helped him to his cabin as Moore went up to the riddled cockpit and took *Obsession*'s wheel. A few minutes later she came up on deck.

"Danforth says to forget the sails and use the motor," she told Moore.

"Works for me," he agreed. "It's been awhile since I did any sailing and it sure as hell wasn't in anything this big!"

As Carla went forward to secure the flapping sails, Moore pointed the yacht for East Point.

"But, sir, they relayed the message," LeFlore protested, "that's all they're required to do!"

"By law, yes," the Old Man answered, "but they have a moral obligation to help anyone in peril on the sea, Marc." McLaughlin looked up at the wooden sailing yacht model on the top shelf of his bookcase. He stood and reached up for the model, taking it gingerly off the shelf.

"You haven't spent much time at sea, have you, Marc?"

LeFlore shook his head. "No, sir, not really," he lied. He hadn't ever been to sea, except for one sport fishing tour off Port Aransas.

McLaughlin held up the model for LeFlore to see. "This was the *Aurora*," he said, his eyes looking past LeFlore, back in time. "We sailed her in the San Francisco–Tahiti race." McLaughlin sat back down at his desk, the model in front of him.

"We were two days out of Papeete," he remembered, "a squall broke the mast and it punched a hole in her as it fell. We just managed to get off a Mayday before she capsized." The Old Man's eyes clouded.

"We clung to her overnight, Marc," he went on. "The next morning, a fisherman picked us up. He had heard the Mayday and sailed his old boat all night, through the squall, to get to us."

"You were all lucky to survive, sir," LeFlore said.

"I didn't say that we all did, Marc," McLaughlin corrected him. "One kid, Anthony, just disappeared during the night. No one saw him go, he just wasn't there the next morning." McLaughlin laced his fingers and held them in front of his face, examining his manicured thumbnails.

"A shark took the guy next to me. His name was Thomas.

He was talking to me and all of a sudden he got this really surprised look on his face. Then he just disappeared. No scream, no nothing. He just popped under the surface." McLaughlin looked up at LeFlore with a stare that made LeFlore's skin crawl.

"His blood soaked my shirt, Marc." McLaughlin stood. "Bob Moore is doing what any good sailor would do. If it costs this company some money, we will pay it and gladly."

"Yes, sir," LeFlore stammered, "I never meant that we shouldn't try to help people in trouble, sir, I just—"

McLaughlin had turned away to look out the window. He waved LeFlore away. LeFlore slipped out of the office, leaving McLaughlin with his memories.

An hour out of East Point, the first sign of trouble appeared. A helicopter swooped low over the yacht, orbiting just above the water. It made half a dozen passes and then headed back toward land.

"I got a bad feeling about that, Carla," Moore observed as the chopper disappeared in the distance.

The sun was setting behind East Point Reef when *Obsession* reached the resort. On the dock, a small knot of people was gathered around the dive boat, the lights from their Minicams flashing back and forth.

"I was afraid of this," Moore sighed as Carla came back up on deck. She had borrowed a pair of baggy shorts and a shirt from Danforth and had her dive suit tied around her waist.

He pointed at the news crews waiting for them. As they neared the dock, they could see Melinda hugging Greg Master and waving to them. She had repaired her hair and makeup.

As Moore cut the engine and let *Obsession* glide up to the pier, the halogen lights flashed onto them.

"Here we go again, Bob"—she smiled as reporters swarmed over the gunwale—"prepare to encourage boarders!" Moore's groan was lost in the first volley of shouted questions.

"Son of a fucking bitch!" Marc LeFlore screamed. As usual, CNN had the first report of Melinda's amazing rescue from bloodthirsty Caribbean pirates. There she was, waving and gushing for the cameras and right behind her was Bob Moore and that slut Carla Fuentes! The blood was pounding so loud in his ears that LeFlore could hardly hear the reporter asking Melinda about her ordeal.

LeFlore hadn't recognized Moore in the helicopter views of the shot-up yacht, but there he was, grimacing and shielding his eyes from the lights.

LeFlore slumped onto his couch and rubbed his forehead. On the screen, Moore was answering questions, giving all the credit to the yacht captain, who was being carried off the yacht on a stretcher, and to the resort staff. Carla Fuentes was smiling and holding the wounded man's hand.

A close-up showed rows of bullet holes and a ragged hole blasted in the yacht's side. Melinda put her arms around Moore and kissed his cheek. Moore looked properly embarrassed, the All-American Hero.

LeFlore snatched the lamp off the table and hurled it at the television screen. It flew to the end of its cord and jerked abruptly to one side, saving the picture tube of the twenty-seven-inch Panasonic.

"Fuck me running!" LeFlore swore. "This time I'm going to have your ass, Moore! I promise you that!"

2

"Did you ever see LeFlore so pissed off?" Carla asked as the plane rotated off the runway. "I thought he was going to bust a gut!"

"I wish he would," Moore sighed. "He is such a dickhead." Moore chuckled and looked over at her. "That's why he wears his ties so tight," Moore quipped, miming tightening a necktie, "keeps the foreskin from sliding up over his face!"

Carla laughed out loud. "You know," she said softly, "I nearly quit when that pinhead got up in our faces."

"Why didn't you?" Moore asked.

"I don't know," she answered, a winsome half smile on her face, "I guess I didn't want to look for some boring desk job." She smiled and squeezed Moore's arm. "Besides, you really know how to show a girl a good time!" It was Moore's turn to laugh. She added, "I'm just sorry we didn't get to dive more."

A round of drinks later, Carla settled into her paperback and Moore stared out the window at the countryside far below. The flight would stop in L.A. to refuel and from there on to Hawaii. In Hawaii, they would change planes for Guam. The day after tomorrow, they would be back on DeepCore.

Tyrone King and Tom Jackson would follow by the end of the week.

Going back to DeepCore had been LeFlore's idea to get them out of the public eye. It had been LeFlore's only good idea.

3

It was a lovely day to be executed.

The sky was a deep blue and the green palms outside Natah's dark cell seemed more vivid than ever before.

Perhaps I have never taken the time to really look at them, he mused.

The salt smell from the ocean breeze briefly dispelled the fetid odor of his cell. A fly buzzed around him, circling for a landing on one of the bloody crusts that covered his filthy shirt.

His interrogators had not been gentle. Dozens of thin, red slashes covered his back and chest. They had hurt at first, especially after his tormentors had splashed him with buckets of seawater. Now, they merely ached, like his arms and his testicles.

His arms were pulled back behind him, tightly bound with wet leather thongs that shrank as they dried, pulling his arms tighter behind him. Tight handcuffs held his wrists. There was little feeling in his hands, not that he could have used them, anyway.

Actually, his testicles did not hurt. He didn't even know for sure where they were. Perhaps Mowati had eaten them. He had heard rumors about the dictator's peculiar habits before. What hurt was the ragged remnants of his scrotum. The little chain saw had not been too precise.

The pains that racked his body were small compared to the pain that tore at his heart. He had not seen or heard of

Alia since they had been arrested. He cringed at the thought of what Mowati must have done to her.

Their crime had been one of the oldest, adultery. But not just adultery, adultery with a wife of the ruler. That made it treason as well.

The memory of their arrest a week before was now just a blur to him. He remembered the loud crack as the door splintered under the boots of the militia. Alia had screamed and screamed as the black-clad policemen had burst into his room and flailed at them with the short bamboo rods. Her white skin had been covered with angry red welts as they dragged her away. He had lost consciousness under the flurry of blows.

He had awakened at his trial. It had been brief. He was convicted of treason, adultery, crimes against God and nature, and a host of lesser charges. The penalty, of course, was death.

The only thing unusual about the trial was that the interrogations came afterward. He had written and signed a lengthy confession in order to get a break from the punishment. Afterward, Mowati himself had arrived to wield the chain saw.

"Alia, my dove," Natah whispered, "I hope you are already dead." He would have cried, but he hadn't had anything to drink for two days. There was no water for the tears.

"Soon," he murmured, "we will be together again. For eternity."

"I hope that is a prayer for your worthless soul!" the harsh voice behind him boomed. Natah turned to face the huge man whose silhouette blocked the cell door. Fashel Jendy had been the prison warden for twenty years. He truly enjoyed his work.

"Prisoner," Jendy shouted, "I am ordered by the holy court to bring you forth this day for execution of your sentence of death. Make peace with Allah in preparation for meeting him!"

Jendy stepped back to let four of his minions into the cell. They pulled Natah away from the window and dragged him down the long, dark corridor out into the prison courtyard. In the center of the courtyard was a riding lawn mower with a small garden cart behind it.

The guards hauled Natah over to the cart and roughly flung him into it. Natah's head slammed into the low railing, cutting his scalp over his right eye. The warm trickle of blood ran down into his eye as they pulled him up on his knees and tied his bound hands to the rail.

"Good-bye, fool"—Jendy laughed as the tiny tractor coughed to life—"next time you want to fuck someone, go fuck yourself!"

The prison guards all laughed at their boss's little joke as the mower towed Natah to the plaza just outside the prison walls.

In the plaza, a huge crowd had gathered to watch the spectacle. Most political executions took place in the prison itself, often in the prisoner's cell, but this was not a simple purge.

Rumors of the arrest had circulated throughout Manawatu. Mowati, humiliated at being cuckolded by a mere clerk, had decided to show the nation what happened to people who insulted him.

Mogador prison had been an old fortress in the days when pirates raided the islands. Now a pirate ruled the islands, and Mogador was a dump for the nation's human trash. Hundreds of Mowati's enemies, both real and imagined, had disappeared behind Mogador's stone walls.

The mower was slow. The crowds that lined the short road between the plaza and the prison were treated to a long look at the man who had seduced a queen. The look was long enough to count the bloody spots on his ripped shirt and observe the thick bloodstain on his crotch.

The cut on his forehead had bled enough to blind his right eye. It was just as well. He really didn't want to see much of what was to come. The crowd was screaming something he could not make out. It seemed to take forever to reach the scaffold erected in the center of the plaza.

The scaffold was a platform about four meters square that stood two meters off the ground. There was a metal bar three meters above the platform, supported by two thick upright I-beams. Two steel cables dangled from the bar.

At the edge of the plaza, Sendu Mowati, President for Life of Manawatu, his four other wives, the judges, and a few court favorites sat on a reviewing stand that faced the scaffold. The wives hid their eyes, their heads bowed. The courtiers seemed amused.

As the mower pulled up to the metal steps that led up to the low platform, Natah could see into the space beneath the platform. It seemed solid. There was no place for a body to drop. He was to be pulled up off the platform! Natah cringed at the thought of strangulation.

At least it won't last for days like the torture, he thought despairingly.

More guards stepped up to untie him and drag him from the cart. They hauled him to his feet and one of them, a tall, powerfully built man, ripped first the tattered shirt and then the crusted pants from his bruised body. The other guards dragged him naked up onto the platform as a pair of public-address speakers atop the scaffold crackled to life. The mower clattered off back to the prison.

"Behold the traitor Natah," the dictator's voice boomed over the speakers, "and witness his punishment!" The guards turned him in all four directions so the crowd could get a better look at the wages of sin. Murmurs and thrills rose up from the crowd as they looked on in fascinated revulsion at his tortured body.

The guards finally dragged him over to the far side of the scaffold, knocked him to his knees, and clipped his hands to a ring set in the floor beneath the scaffold. Natah looked up at the two hooks that dangled overhead from thin steel cables, afraid to wonder about their purpose.

"Animals," Natah spat at the onlookers, "you will be next!" The crowd roared its approval of his spirit.

The sun was already high but the strong, cool breeze off the ocean kept the heat at bay. From the platform, Natah could see the thick bank of clouds that hovered on the horizon. There was a storm approaching, a big one.

It was no concern of his, of course, he would not be alive by the time it reached Manawatu.

Natah tried to focus on the blue sky and the cool breeze to keep his mind off the torture to come. He remembered his first meeting with Alia, when he had fallen hopelessly, desperately in love with her, knowing that love to be forbidden.

A shy, beautiful girl from a tiny village, she had only recently been married to Mowati. Natah's job had been to school her in protocol and court manners. She had been a bright, eager pupil, so serious about her lessons. She hardly knew the dictator. Her father had readily agreed to her marriage, to refuse the dictator was to invite the destruction of your whole family. Better to lose a daughter than the entire household.

At first she had been happy in the palace. Mowati was rarely interested in her and she took little part in the jealous intrigues of the other wives. She preferred the comfort of her books, and of her tutor.

They had first become intimate after one of Mowati's drunken rages. He had beaten Alia and forced himself on her. Natah's attempt to comfort her led to physical comforting as well.

After that, the court gossips had planted the seeds of jealousy in the dictator's mind. Their arrest had been inevitable.

Natah's musing was interrupted by the mower's roar. He strained at his bonds to see it. She was in the cart. His heart sank. Mowati would force one to watch the other die.

"Please, forgiving God," Natah begged, "let me die first. I cannot bear to watch her suffer!"

The crowd roared as the mower pulled up alongside the scaffold. From where he knelt, Natah could not see Alia. The speaker came back to life.

"Here is his accomplice, Alia Pinqual," Mowati's voice boomed, using Alia's family name. "She will share his fate!"

A moment later Alia appeared on the platform. She was being dragged between the same two guards. They dragged her over next to him and pulled her handcuffed arms up in front of her, slipping the metal hook under the chain that connected the cuffs.

They stripped her then, standing behind her and ripping the thin shift away. The crowd roared again. This time there was another tone to the noise, a dirty, snickering sound that turned Natah's stomach.

Her naked skin seemed even whiter in the bright sunlight. Her head hung down on her chest and her long black hair, now tangled and filthy, obscured her face. Her thin body was covered with dark slashes that stood out against her alabaster skin. Her small breasts, so smooth and firm before, were now masses of huge dark bruises. Bloody crusts covered both her tiny nipples.

Natah's spirit plummeted. She had suffered as much as he had.

"Alia," he whispered. She seemed to hear and turned her face to him. Natah choked on his scream. Her face was so swollen it was almost round. Dark bruises shadowed both cheeks and her full lower lip was split. Those wounds were not the worst, though.

To insure that she could not look away or close her eyes to block out her tormentor's face, her eyelids had been cut. She stared at him with blank red eyes that tore at his soul.

The guards unfastened him from the ring and pulled him up onto his feet. They stepped around behind him and slipped the hook through his handcuffs.

"No!" Natah begged as the gibbet grew taut, pulling him up by his arms. Pain shot up into his shoulders as his arms were forced up. One of the guards knelt and slipped a loop around his feet, securing them to the ring in the platform. If he stood on tiptoes, he could almost relieve the pain in his arm sockets, but he knew he could not stand that way for long. If he could not stand, his own weight would dislocate his arms from their sockets. He prayed that death would come sooner than that. Mowati's voice boomed out again over the loudspeaker.

"The traitors before you have been condemned by holy courts for crimes against God and the Republic," he shouted. "They are sentenced to die for their crimes. Let their punishment serve as a warning to those who would betray God and the Protector of the Faithful!"

There was no noise now from the crowd. Natah raised his head to look toward the reviewing stand. He could only see half a meter in front of the platform's edge. The crowd parted and Mowati stepped up in front of the scaffold. One of the guards handed him a long stick of some sort. Mowati looked up into Natah's ruined face.

"Here," he said, his voice ringing out over the speakers, "taste now the flames that await you both in hell!"

Mowati held the stick to one side where a guard stood waiting. Orange flame suddenly flickered at the end of the stick. Mowati stepped back and thrust the stick under the scaffold. Only then did it occur to Natah that they were to be burned alive.

"In the name of God, Sendu," he screamed, "have mercy! Burn me but not her!" The crackling sound below him and the sudden rush of smoke around them was his only answer.

Natah thought he heard the crowd roar again, but all he could really hear were Alia's exhausted screams. He twisted to look at her, a spear of pain stabbing his agonized shoulders.

Flames licked up through the boards beneath them, burning their bare feet. Alia was twisting now, pulling her feet up from the burning platform. Natah shut his eyes tight to block out the sight, knowing that she could not.

He screamed as the flames charred the skin of his feet and kept screaming until the smoke and flames killed him five minutes later. By that time, Alia was already dead.

4

Above them, the hurricane raged.

"What's it look like up there, Number One?" Titus Merganthal, captain of the HMS *Revenge*, asked.

"The same, Skipper," Corbin "Corky" O'Connor, the executive officer, answered. "Still got hundred-mile-an-hour winds and increasing. It hasn't moved all day."

"Glad we're not in a destroyer, eh?" Merganthal quipped.

"Too bloody right about that, sir!" O'Connor agreed. The typhoon had come up in their path two days ago. It seemed to be following them on their patrol route, though a bit more slowly. Two hundred feet below the surface, the *Revenge* was spared the blasting wind and towering seas above. *Revenge* was monitoring the storm with instruments.

"Are we getting any navigation readings through it?" Merganthal asked, scanning the readouts that showed the old sub's depth and position.

"Pretty well, sir," O'Connor answered, "sometimes the static is too bad to get a good fix, but we just keep trying until we get one."

"Right," Merganthal said, "carry on then. I'll be in the wardroom."

"Aye, aye, sir."

Merganthal was in the passageway when the intercom squawked to life.

"Captain to the bridge," O'Connor's voice crackled, "sonar contact."

"What have you got, Jefferies," Merganthal asked as he

stepped back into the command center and peered over the sonar operator's shoulder. The top of the yellow screen was dotted with tiny red blips.

"Don't know, sir," Jefferies answered, looking up at the captain, "it's a strange pattern. It's not moving, but it's not stationary either. I mean, the images move slightly, but not in a linear pattern."

"What's its depth?" Merganthal asked.

"Just subsurface down to one hundred feet," the sonarman answered.

The captain's face suddenly went white. "Mines!" he shouted. He turned to the intercom box.

"Helm, this is the captain!" he snapped. "All stop! Repeat, all stop emergency!"

"A mine field, sir?" the sonarman asked, incredulous. "What would a mine field be doing here in the middle of nowhere?"

"I don't know, son," Merganthal replied, studying the flickering images on the scope, "but there they are. I haven't seen a regular tethered mine field in years, no, in decades. Everyone uses those damn encapsulated mines now. The last bunch that had any tethered mines was Iran, a few years ago."

The *Revenge* was slowing rapidly now. Merganthal held on to the sonarman's chair to keep his balance.

"The hell of it is," the skipper went on, "a big storm like this one can literally pick up a mine field and drop it somewhere else."

"Doesn't that set off the mines?" Jefferies asked.

"Sometimes, sometimes not."

A dull boom reverberated through the hull, the sound distant and distorted. "When it does"—Merganthal pointed upward—"it sounds like that." He turned to the ladder that led up to the control center.

"Keep a sharp eye on 'em, Jefferies," he told the suddenly frightened sonarman. "Let me know if anything changes or they move any closer."

In the control center, the exec and a dozen troubled seamen were waiting for him.

"What in the name of Christ was that, sir?" O'Connor asked, his face alarmingly pale.

"A mine," Merganthal replied. "There seems to be a swarm of them up ahead. We need to move at a right angle to them and skirt the field."

"Whose mines are they, sir?" Davenport, the helmsman, asked.

"I don't really know," Merganthal answered, "I just know we need to get around them, wide around. Come left to one-eight-zero."

"Aye, sir," Davenport answered, "one-eight-zero."

"Corky," Merganthal said to the exec, "better call action stations and rig the boat for depth charge, just in case."

"Aye, sir," O'Connor replied, reaching up for the intercom switch. He spoke into the microphone grill.

"Action stations! Rig for depth charge!" he barked. "Action stations, rig for depth charge!" A klaxon sounded, followed by the sound of running feet.

"Better safe than sorry, eh, sir?" O'Connor asked, "I remember—"

A loud metallic bang echoed through the boat. On the sonar deck below, the sonarman on the hydrophone yelled as the object hit the hydrophone, sending a painful boom through the sensitive receiver.

"Dammit!" the man cursed. "What the hell was—"

The *Revenge* shook as a huge explosion erupted on the bow.

"Emergency blow forward," Merganthal shouted, clutching the periscope to keep on his feet. Compressed air hissed into the empty ballast spaces in *Revenge*'s forward sections. The deck below their feet tilted up sharply. O'Connor fell against the periscope, grabbing at it to keep from falling the length of the command center. The lights went off, then flickered back on.

"Emergency power!" Merganthal screamed into the intercom. "All ahead flank! One hundred percent power on the reactor!"

"Full ahead, aye," a voice from engineering answered, "one hundred percent power on the reactor—"

Another boom shook the sub. "Explosion!" the voice from engineering screamed. "Hull rupture! Taking water in after engineering spa—" The intercom suddenly went silent.

The helmsman spun around in his seat, his eyes wide with fear.

"Captain," he shouted, "speed is slowing. We've lost power!"

"Engineering!" Merganthal shouted into the silent intercom. "Engineering! Full power! Do you hear me? Full power!"

"Speed is zero!" the helmsman called. "Sir, we're sliding backward."

"O'Connor," Merganthal snapped, "get down to engineering and get us some power quick!"

O'Connor was on the stairs when the *Revenge* slid slowly backward into the rock plateau beneath them, buckling the tough steel skin and destroying any hope that the *Revenge* would move again under its own power.

Merganthal could not hear the screams of his sailors as they died in those spaces aft of the reactor room, crushed by the ice-cold Pacific.

5

Sendu Mowati was depressed.

The execution had been a great spectacle, but he was left now with a sad feeling, not the elation he usually felt when he sent a traitor to hell.

Still, it was hard to kill a wife, particularly a new, pretty one. It was hard to kill your own brother, too.

Ordinarily, he loved to hear condemned prisoners beg for mercy. He never gave it, but it felt good to hear them beseech him. His brother's pleas seemed to haunt him now.

At least that little bitch had kept her mouth shut, he groused, except to scream. Her screams echoed through his head, now, too.

"Damn the two of them!" he cursed. "First they insult me with their whorish behavior, and now they haunt me! Damn them!"

He had stayed on the reviewing stand until the flames had risen up over their heads and the screaming had stopped.

Now, back in his apartment in the palace to change from his formal uniform back into his fatigues, he felt a surge of depression.

Even from the grave they can mock you, he thought bitterly.

A knock at the door interrupted his brooding.

"Come!"

A nervous young lieutenant opened the door and slipped inside.

"Excellency," he began, his voice cracking, "we intercepted this message a few moments ago!" He stepped forward and thrust a message sheet out in front of him.

Mowati took the paper and read the message.

"You are sure this is not some trick?" he asked the young officer.

"We believe it is authentic, Exalted One," the lieutenant answered.

Mowati stood looking at the paper for a moment, then waved the young man away.

"Excellent, Lieutenant, return to your post," he ordered. The lieutenant saluted and vanished.

A wide smile split Sendu Mowati's dark face.

Allah had taken a wife and a brother from him this day, but had now given him the world in return.

"Allahu Akbar," Mowati shouted, "God is truly great!"

6

Bob Moore's head dropped forward, his forehead bouncing off the video monitor with a muffled *bong*. Behind him, Tyrone King chuckled.

"Noddin' off, boss?" King asked.

Moore rubbed his eyes and stretched. "Me?" he answered. "No way! There's nothing like sitting in the dark watching a big hose suck mud up off the bottom to keep me on the edge of my seat!" He shifted to look back at King. "Hey, underwater mining is my life!"

King, barely visible in the gloomy interior of the control room, chuckled again. "We need to get you topside again," King observed, "sounds like you're coming down with 'boredom of the deep'!"

"No shit!" Moore answered, rising from the small chair to stand up in the big cylinder that was one leg of the starfish-shaped installation.

"How long are we in the doghouse for, anyway?" King asked. "I mean, you didn't actually shoot LeFlore or anything, you just got in his face."

"I told you before," Moore answered, "LeFlore didn't send us back, the Old Man did. He thought we'd be better off down here until the heat died down. The Old Man is playing along with the State Department."

"Yeah, I know the drill," King replied in a singsong voice, "we don't know who they were."

"Right," Moore agreed, "and here a thousand feet below the surface of the Pacific, we are unavailable for comment."

"Well," King observed, "they sure as shit don't need us to protect DeepCore."

Moore chuckled. The U.S. Navy had sent two more Los Angeles–class subs to protect the stricken USS *Houston*, which still lay on the bottom next to DeepCore. Half of SEAL team six, the Navy's elite antiterrorist unit, had accompanied the subs. They were now on DeepCore. Moore and the others from UnderSea Corporation's Security Department were completely unnecessary.

To earn their keep, Moore had volunteered them to replace the deep-sea divers who had been killed in the attack. Now, he and King were operating a robot mining unit on an underwater atoll two hundred miles from DeepCore. Carla Fuentes and Tom Jackson were on their way out to relieve them after their two-week rotation. Moore had left Elgin Bickerstaff at UnderSea's corporate headquarters, primarily because Bickerstaff irritated Marc LeFlore so badly.

The other Security team member, Larry Ramos, was still recovering from his wounds. He was back on DeepCore now, manning the security desk and trying to impress the SEALs with his tales of manly valor.

"I'll be glad when Tom and Carla get here," King said. "This place is more boring than a Baptist picnic."

"I hear that," Moore commiserated. "Next time, we'll bring some videotapes, pornos maybe."

The clatter of the computer printer in the center hub interrupted.

"Wonderful," Moore moaned, "this better not be Carla with some excuse for why they're not coming!"

He walked back to get the message off the printer. The words MAYDAY MESSAGE stood out in bold letters.

"Oh, shit, Ty," Moore called over his shoulder, "we got a Mayday!"

King jumped up from his screen and joined Moore in the center hub.

Moore tore the message from the printer and read it aloud.

"Mayday, HMS *Revenge*. Request immediate assistance." An eight-digit map coordinate followed.

"This came in digital over the emergency channel," King observed, reading the code at the top of the printout. "Wonder why it quit so quick?"

Moore shook his head. "Maybe the storm. Anyway, we're close to these guys, we need to do something." He stepped over to the communication console and switched it to transmit.

"DeepCore shuttle, this is Rock Sucker. Come in, Carla."

A moment later Carla's distorted voice came over the speaker.

"Go ahead, Sucker," she answered.

"Pedal to the metal, Gretel," Moore said, "we got some folks in trouble near here. We need your sub."

"On the way," Carla answered, "ETA two hours."

"Roger, Carla. Two hours," Moore acknowledged, "Rock Sucker out." He hung the microphone back on the console.

"Well, HMS *Revenge*," he said to the printout, "hang in there, baby." He turned to King. "Let's shut down the mine and dig up whatever rescue stuff we've got. I want to shove off as soon as Carla and Tom get here."

"Got it," King answered. Moore turned to the main control console. He switched the robot mining gear to STANDBY, then a minute later shut them down completely. As the hum and whine of the robot equipment faded, an uneasy silence fell over the complex.

While King collected the emergency gear, Moore dug through a cabinet under the work desk, looking for the Jane's listing of the world's ships.

7

"Come on, Carla!" Moore shouted as King and Jackson stored the last of the rescue equipment in the small sub. Carla reappeared, zipping up her snug coveralls.

"Excuse me," she answered, "I had to pee!"

She climbed up into the little shuttle sub. Moore climbed up behind her, pulling shut and dogging the pressure door to the complex first, then dropping the sub's hatch shut and locking it.

"Hatch secure," he called to Tom Jackson, who was in the pilot's seat.

"Roger," Jackson answered, "flooding skirt now." A moment later Jackson spoke again. "Skirt flooded, soft seal. Disengaging." The little submarine rocked as it popped loose from the mining complex.

"You got a heading yet?" Moore asked as he slid up behind Jackson.

"Locked in," Jackson answered, patting the onboard computer. "If we just leave it alone, this little guy will take us right there."

The shuttle sub whined off toward the coordinates where the *Revenge* lay waiting.

"What do we have left, Number One?" Merganthal asked.

"Precious little, sir," O'Connor answered. "Forward torpedo is taking water, but not too much, engineering is flooded, the power is off, missile room is still dry. The reactor shut itself down."

"Casualties?"

O'Connor paused. "A lot, sir," he answered. "When we hit, we lost nearly everyone in engineering and in the aft accommodations."

The captain's head dropped. "How many?" he asked, his eyes closed.

"Forty or so dead, thirty-five injured," O'Connor estimated. "Most of the injuries are broken bones and head injuries from the impact."

"God," Merganthal moaned, holding his head with his hand. The gesture brought his arm up. O'Connor noticed the blood on the captain's arm.

"Are you hurt, sir?" he asked.

The captain shook his head. "Just a nick," he answered, "it's nothing. Did we manage to fire the buoy before we hit?"

"Just before," O'Connor replied, "it should be on top by now."

If that storm hasn't wrecked it, both men thought.

"So, what is our situation?" Merganthal asked.

"We have air for as much as seventy-two hours," O'Connor answered. "More if we divert some of the battery power to the scrubbers. There is no radiation leak, and we have plenty of food. The only pressing problem is the wounded. Some of them will die if we don't get help soon."

Both men understood that possibility was remote.

"Very good, Number One," Merganthal said, "make the wounded comfortable and see what communications are still possible. We may be here awhile."

Or forever, both men knew.

8

Fleet Admiral Pyotr Ganilev smiled as he looked at the satellite photo. The typhoon's white, circular swirl covered most of the photo. On the clear acetate overlay, a red circle marked a spot one hundred miles off the coast of Manawatu, which was outlined in green.

"The transmission was brief, Comrade Fleet Admiral," an excited Signal captain standing nearby blurted. "The transmission was interrupted as if the equipment had been damaged. We were able to get a fix on it, though."

"Horocho," Ganilev murmured in the deep voice others had compared to distant thunder. "Excellent!" He stood and smiled.

"You and your group have done well, Captain," he complimented the beaming officer. "Classify this information at the highest level and transmit it to the submarine closest to the location."

"That would be the *Ulan Bator,* Comrade Fleet Admiral," the captain said brightly, pleased with himself for determining the fleet vessels in the area before delivering the message.

"What is your name, Captain?" Ganilev asked.

"Borskov, Comrade Fleet Admiral," the man replied, "Dimitri Borskov."

"I will remember your efficiency, Captain Borskov," Ganilev said softly.

"I serve the Soviet Union!" Borskov blurted. He saluted and left, smiling broadly.

A British missile sub down, Ganilev mused. A wonderful, if fleeting, opportunity!

If no one else had heard the SOS, they could conceivably recover the boat itself and its missiles! At the very least, they could reap a publicity coup by rescuing the British crew.

In any event, it was the chance for him to look good for the pencil pushers in Moscow. In these days of economic restructuring and chronic public unrest, Moscow loved a hero as never before.

This time, he would be that hero.

The warmth spread down Vasili Ivask from his face onto his chest. After eight months of Aleutian patrols, the warm sun was a treat. His skin was as white as a fish's belly.

After eight months down here, he smiled, I'll look like that *Chernozhoph* that sailed with us last year. Halle Miriam, an Ethiopian officer, had sailed on one voyage as part of an officer exchange. Miriam's skin was so black it was almost purple. He had been worse than useless. Ethiopia had no submarines. Miriam had been underfoot all the time and panicky whenever they were submerged.

The captain had burned the black man's bedding after he had left the ship.

The *Ulan Bator* was ten days out of Cam Ranh Bay, Vietnam, on its second South Pacific patrol. Since the disintegration of the Warsaw Pact, the Soviets had increased their presence in the Pacific. The *Ulan Bator* patrolled the Pacific, popping up here and there to remind the U.S. Navy that the South Pacific was not just a large American lake.

In two hours, they would rendezvous with a tanker, refuel and start back west on the final leg of the patrol.

I will go up to Vung Tau after we return, he decided, and see if it is such a resort after all. Perhaps the women there will be more attractive than the slatterns who hang around

Cam Ranh. Perhaps there will be—

"Diving stations!" the captain's voice boomed over the squawk box. The dive warning horn sounded. Ivask sprang to his feet, hastily buttoning his shirt as the two machinists who were working on the attack periscope scrambled to replace the periscope lens cover. Below the long sail, the blue Pacific water began to lap over the deck.

"Hurry!" Ivask suggested to the two technicians. They ignored him, intent on bolting down the cover plate. The water was halfway up the sail when the last bolt was snug. The two machinists dropped through the hatch with Ivask right behind them. He pulled the hatch chain, slamming the heavy pressure hatch above him. Valnikov, the senior enlisted man on the boat, dogged the hatch shut.

"Comrade Senior Lieutenant," Minsk, one of the machinists, blurted, "we were not finished! The attack periscope is not operational!"

"So noted, machinist," Ivask snapped, "assume your diving station!"

"Just so!" Minsk answered. He and the other machinist disappeared down the ladder to the deck below.

"Lieutenant Ivask to the wardroom!" the intercom blared. Ivask followed the two machinists down the ladder, headed forward toward the officers' mess hall.

In the wardroom, the other officers were already assembled. Captain Gregoriy, looking startled and a bit more rumpled than Ivask had ever seen him, was holding a sheet of the flimsy paper from the communications room.

"Now that we're all here," Gregoriy began, "we have received the following order from Pacific Fleet." He held up the slick paper and read the decoded message. "Proceed at best submerged speed to assist HMS *Revenge*, reported down in Area Gamma. Further instructions to follow." The captain looked up. "That is all of the message."

"Comrade Captain, Area Gamma is a very large place," Antonov, the navigator, observed, "nearly two thousand square kilometers." Glances were exchanged all around. "In addition," Antonov went on, "there is at this time a typhoon parked right over it. Winds are up to one hundred fifty kilometers an hour and fifteen-meter seas. The storm is almost stationary."

"That explains the order to run submerged," one of the other officers observed.

"What is does not explain is why we did not hear the SOS ourselves," Markovic, the communications officer, countered.

"We do not need explanations, comrades," the captain interrupted, "we have our orders and we will comply with them. Return to your stations and make best speed to the area."

"Comrade Captain," Ivask asked quickly, "what about the refueling tanker?"

"We have more than enough fuel to reach the area," the captain retorted. "We will refuel after we see to the *Revenge*."

Ivask did not press the issue.

This cruise is becoming anything but routine, he mused as he and the others filed out of the wardroom and returned to the task of running the *Ulan Bator*.

Mohammad Patno, captain of the *19th of January*, Manawatu's only submarine, stared at the short printout, the two creases between his bushy eyebrows deepening.

"This was the entire message?" he asked the radioman.

"It is, Captain," the young ensign answered, "I have already asked for confirmation."

Ordinarily, Patno would have berated the inexperienced ensign for anticipating an order. On his submarine, he gave the orders, no one else. Today, though, he would let it go.

This enigmatic order was of more concern than a minor infraction of discipline.

The message was brief. It read: PROCEED NORTH TO THE LINE OF DEATH AND DEFEND THE REPUBLIC AGAINST ALL MARITIME ENEMIES, SURFACE AND SUBMERGED. What that meant, exactly, was unclear.

What enemies? Patno wondered as he gave the order to turn north, we are not at war. We have no maritime enemies. Even if we did, that typhoon would do an excellent job of keeping them at bay.

There was obviously more to this than the order itself. Hopefully, there would be clarifications later. Their commander in chief was frequently erratic, but there was usually method to his madness.

This submarine was the living proof of that. Named for the date that Sendu Mowati had seized power, it had been secretly purchased from the Indonesians two years before. A German Type 209, it was one of the best nonnuclear subs available.

The Indonesians had reported the sub sunk in order to conceal the sale from the nosy Americans and Europeans. The regular shipments of spare parts and torpedoes were hidden in other orders for the Indonesian Navy.

The *19th of January*'s eight torpedo tubes were loaded with heavy German SUT torpedoes, effective against both surface ships and submarines. In addition to those in the tubes, there were six reloads.

The sub was quiet and could remain submerged for long periods. Its large single prop could propel it at speeds up to twenty-two knots underwater.

"Captain," Lt. Eli Askart, the executive officer, interrupted Patno's speculation, "we will be heading right into the worst of the typhoon. I doubt that we will be able to reach the Line of Death on the surface."

"Then we will proceed submerged," the captain shot back. "Where is the weather chart?" He followed Askart back to the navigation table.

"The eye of the storm is here," Askart explained. "It is moving north very slowly."

"How long will it take us to reach the Line of Death?" Patno asked.

"Five hours, thirty minutes," Askart replied.

"Where will the storm center be at that time?" Patno inquired.

"Just beyond the Line of Death," Askart answered, suddenly realizing his captain's plan. "We can surface in the eye of the storm to recharge our batteries."

"Exactly"—Patno smiled—"we will run on the surface until the sea is too rough. See to it that the batteries are at maximum charge."

"Aye, aye," Askart answered as Patno turned back toward the message center.

"How far are we, Carla?" Moore asked, watching the battery readouts. They had been under way for hours, pushing the shuttle sub to reach the stricken British submarine.

"Should be there anytime, now," she answered, "if their position was correct."

"Ty, get on the sonar," Moore said to King, who had come forward to look out the front observation bubble, "we're going to be looking deep."

"Not too deep, I hope," the big man answered, "this baby ain't no DSRV, you know."

"I do indeed," Moore replied. The Navy's Deep Submergence Rescue Vehicles could operate in water five thousand feet deep. Their small shuttle could only handle a fraction of that depth.

"Wonder what that storm is doing topside?" King asked

Tom Jackson as the sonar warmed up.

"I don't know," Jackson replied, stretching, "but I'm glad we're not up there!"

The sonar sweep began, probing the depths below with sound waves that would reveal any obstacles below. Each pulse rang through the sub's hull with a high, bell-like tone.

"Boss, you know that this little sonar is not really designed for this," King called forward to Moore. "That sub is rubber-coated so it doesn't reflect."

"I know, Ty, but it's all we've got!" Moore answered. "Just keep a close eye on it. You probably won't get much of a return."

"Partial power restored, Captain," O'Connor reported. "We have the reactor at ten percent power, just enough to run the emergency generators and the air scrubbers."

"Thank you, Number One," Merganthal answered. He was in the cramped sick bay, watching the ship's doctor treat the many injured men. Two of them had died from head wounds. The others were mostly broken bones, broken when the ship slammed into the narrow plateau. Merganthal had come down to tell them the situation and try to keep their spirits up.

It had been hours since the sub had hit the wandering mines. There was no way to know if the emergency buoy was transmitting or if their SOS message on the emergency net had reached anyone. Their next scheduled transmission was not for another twenty-two hours. They might not even be missed until then.

O'Connor's voice crackled over the intercom speaker. "Captain," the executive officer shouted, "we have active sonar pinging! Someone's looking for us!"

"I'll be right there, Number One!" Merganthal answered. He turned to the wounded men. "Hear that, lads?" he shouted. "We're rescued! You'll be in hospital soon."

A ragged cheer followed him up the ladder to the command center.

O'Connor was waiting by the passive sonar display. The midships hydrophone array, the only hydrophone still operable, was picking up a thin, high-pitched ringing.

"It isn't a military set, sir," O'Connor observed, "probably a research vessel or even a whaler."

"I don't care if it's your aunt Tilly in a rowboat," Merganthal answered, "I'm damn glad to hear 'em! Can we give them an answering ping?"

"I don't know, sir," O'Connor explained. "The forward hydrophones are gone, I haven't tried the active since we shut everything down." He nodded to Jefferies, the sonar operator. Jefferies switched on the set, waited a few seconds for it to warm up, then pressed the red button that manually activated the powerful Type 2001 active sonar.

A loud ping echoed through the hull.

"We're here, mates," O'Connor shouted to the searchers, "come and get us!"

"This sonar uses a lot of battery power, Bob," Tom Jackson reminded Moore. "If we use it for very long, we're going to get pretty low on juice."

"I know, Tom," Moore answered, "but there's not much point in coming out here if we're not going to look for these guys." Moore looked over his shoulder. "Besides, those guys may not have much time left."

Jackson nodded. "I hope—"

A loud *ka-bong!* interrupted him.

"Ho-ly shit!" King shouted from the sub's cabin. "That wasn't our set. That's some big sonofabitch!"

"Looks like we've hit pay dirt," Moore observed. "Let's find 'em and get them out of that sub."

9

"We will be in the typhoon's eye in two minutes, Captain," Askart reported.

"Very well, Lieutenant," Patno answered, "go to battle stations."

"Sir," Askart asked, "who are we looking for?"

"I do not know," Patno answered, "but we will be ready for them. Prepare to transmit a message to base. Say that we are on station and await further orders."

"Aye," Askart answered, switching off the intercom.

Patno sat at the tiny desk in his cabin, looking at the pictures taped on the bulkhead above it. There was a photo of a very young Patno in his school uniform with his parents at graduation. That had been in the old days when Manawatu had been a British protectorate aspiring to Commonwealth status.

Another photo showed Patno in a British ensign's uniform, standing next to the huge bulbous sonar dome on the deck of an old Oberon-class submarine. Patno had been thrilled when the Royal Navy had accepted him to submarine school. The *Orpheus* had been new then, the pride of the British submarine fleet.

He had returned to Manawatu in '74 to help build a navy for the newly independent republic. He had met Mowati a year later. The only other picture on the wall was one of Walli Buto Mowati's predecessor, christening the first of Manawatu's coastal patrol boats. Standing off to one side in the photo was then Captain Mowati. He seemed to be staring at Buto.

Who could have known then that in a few years Mowati would seize power, kill Buto, and declare himself President for Life. Since then, the islands had been ruled by force, fear, and hunger.

The people of Manawatu had traded their colonial masters for a ruthless homegrown dictator.

Patno remembered a line from an old Kipling poem he had read during his schooling in England.

"But a servant when he reigneth is more than ever slave."

At the time, the poem had insulted him, yet now it seemed prophetic.

Patno's reminiscences were interrupted by the intercom.

"Captain," Askart reported, "we have received another message from our base."

"On my way," Patno answered, rising and sweeping the past from his mind.

In the command center, Askart was waiting with the flimsy printout. His expression was one of amazed confusion. He handed Patno the coded message without comment.

The first message had been ambiguous, but this one was quite specific, though unbelievable. It read: SEARCH FOR BRITISH SUBMARINE SUNK IN AREA DESIGNATED. WHEN FOUND, REPORT FOR FURTHER INSTRUCTIONS. CAUTION! ANY OTHER VESSELS FOUND IN AREA MUST BE ASSUMED HOSTILE. ENGAGE ON CONTACT.

The search area designated was not large. The nearest coordinate was an hour away. Patno looked up at his executive officer's expression of disbelief.

"Send an acknowledgment," he said as calmly as he could. "Make best speed to the search area."

"Shall we stay at battle stations, Captain?" Askart asked.

Patno looked at the row of faces in the command center. All were turned to him, waiting.

"We will remain at battle stations until we—" he began.

"Sonar contact!" Eli Kandar, the sonar operator, shouted. "Subsurface! Heavy ping!"

"We will remain at battle stations, Mr. Askart." The captain smiled, raising one bushy eyebrow.

The sonar operator interrupted again.

"New contact," he barked, "moving at high speed!"

"Prepare to engage the moving target, Mr. Askart."

Askart's expression of disbelief deepened, a trace of fear widening his dark eyes.

"What have you got, Sonar?" Gregoriy asked.

"Active ping, Comrade Captain," the sonarman replied, "range fifty kilometers, bearing two-one-four."

"Come right to two-one-four," Gregoriy ordered. "Sonar, give me an identification as soon as possible!"

"Processing now, Comrade Captain," the sonarman answered.

"So, Ivask," Gregoriy chortled, "we have found them easily! How thoughtful of them to signal us!"

The printer next to the sonarman clattered. He turned in his chair and ripped off the strip of paper.

"Target classified, Comrade Captain," he reported. "British Type 2001 active sonar."

"Excellent!" Gregoriy snapped. "Ivask, you have the ship. I will be in the radio room." The captain disappeared down the ladder, leaving Ivask in command.

The sonar pings and returns were almost simultaneous now.

"Hit the lights," Moore said, peering out through the thick Lexan bubble. King reached past Moore and flipped the switch. At first, there was no real difference. The sunless depths soaked up the light like some aquatic black hole.

"Got to be here somewhere," King insisted. "Sonar says we're right on top of it."

"We'll find it," Moore answered. "It's too big to miss." The words were barely out of his mouth when the huge black hull seemed to rise up into the lights below them.

"Goddammit!" Moore swore. "Scared me to death!" The little sub's lights played along the huge hull. An immense jagged hole yawned under them, sucking the light into the sub's ruptured skin.

"Holy shit, Bob," King exclaimed, "that looks like a torpedo hit!"

"No wonder they didn't get off much of a message," Moore agreed, "they probably sunk like a rock!"

"I wonder how many are still alive?" Carla asked from behind them.

"One anyway," King answered, "the guy who pinged us."

As they slowly swam down the length of the hull, a large circular hatch entered the pool of light.

"Torpedo hatch," Moore observed, "there should be a rescue hatch abaft of it somewhere." A minute later a smaller hatch appeared under the work sub's lights.

"Bingo!" Moore announced. He slowed the sub, letting its inertia guide it over the opening. Tom Jackson was peering down through the observation window in the bottom hatch.

"Easy, easy," he coaxed, "come left a little." Moore twisted the pistol grip control. Thrusters on the bow and stern pushed the little sub sideways.

"Okay, easy does it," Jackson guided. "Now!"

Moore opened the free flood holes atop the little sub, letting it sink onto the deck of the sunken missile boat. His little sub listed as it made contact. Jackson called out as the two subs touched.

"Soft seal," he said, flipping the lever that would pull out some of the water in the skirt and use the water pressure outside to secure the small sub to the larger one.

"Hard seal," Jackson hollered as the work sub firmed up its footing on the big missile sub's deck. Moore shut down the motors and came back to the hatch. The others were clustered around it, trying to get a look through the little window.

"Ready to crack it?" Moore asked. Jackson looked up and rolled his eyes.

"I guess so," he answered nervously.

"Okay," Moore said, reaching for a brass hammer clipped to the wall near the hatch. He used the hammer to tap the lugs that held the hatch shut. The first came loose easily. He had to hit the second one several times to get it to move. When it did, the hatch popped up a few inches, then banged back down. Moore pulled it all the way up and King locked it open.

Below, the wet, rubberized hull of the stricken sub gleamed in the shuttle's lights.

"Let's say hello," Moore suggested. He leaned down and hit the hull twice with his hammer. The blows resulted only in muffled bongs.

Moore was drawing back the hammer for another rap when the hatch suddenly tipped up and a pale face peered up at them from below as a blast of fetid air rushed up out of the big sub. Moore reacted to the ugly smell with an equally ugly face.

"Nice to see you, too, darling," the pale face said. "What's all this then, eh?"

Moore wiped the grimace off his face and grinned down at the man. "We were in the neighborhood," he answered, "thought we'd drop by for tea."

The man's face split into a wide smile.

"Permission to come aboard?" Moore asked formally. The man snapped a British palm-out salute.

"Gladly granted. Welcome aboard Her Majesty's Ballistic

Missile Submarine *Revenge*, Captain Merganthal commanding."

Moore swung his feet down through the hatch and grabbed the handholds inside, letting himself drop into the sub.

"Bob Moore, UnderSea Corporation," he replied, sticking out his hand. The English officer took it and shook it firmly.

"Corbin O'Connor, executive officer," the man introduced himself, "damn glad you're here!" O'Connor looked up as another pair of tennis shoes appeared through the hatch. Carla dropped down next to the two men. O'Connor's eyes grew wide as his gaze swept down to Carla's cleavage, several inches of which were visible above her jumpsuit's zipper.

"Carla Fuentes," she said, dropping her head down to his line of sight. He immediately looked back up at her face, a look of true disbelief washing across his. She stuck out her hand and O'Connor took it.

"Charmed, I'm sure," he said emphatically. She smiled in return.

O'Connor hardly noticed the two other Americans who dropped down into the sub. King and Jackson introduced themselves.

"Of course," O'Connor replied, "thank you all for coming after us!" He pointed down the narrow passageway. "Please come this way."

In the red-lit command center, a cluster of sailors waited, their faces tight with fear. One of them, a small, thin man with gray wisps of hair over his temples, stepped forward, a large smile on his face.

"Welcome aboard the *Revenge,*" he said, shaking their hands eagerly, "I'm Captain Merganthal." When he got to Carla's hand, he smiled broadly. "We had about given up hope," Merganthal went on. "We didn't know if any of our signals got through."

"One did," Tom Jackson answered.

"Captain," O'Connor interrupted, "I'd like to start transferring our injured to the rescue sub."

"Of course, Number One," Merganthal answered.

"Carla," Moore said, turning to his crew, "you guys give them a hand."

The four of them had just started down the passageway when the sonarman leaned forward, holding his headphones and staring at a thin line on the sonar screen.

"Hydrophone contact," the man called, "submarine."

"Well, Mr. Moore," Merganthal observed, "you seem to be the harbinger of rescue."

Moore looked confused and a bit concerned.

"I hope so," he said, "but I don't know of any other rescue vessels but ours."

"Indeed?" Merganthal answered. He turned to the sonarman.

"Jefferies, can you classify that contact?"

"I'll try, Captain."

"This new arrival may make your little sub redundant," Merganthal said brightly.

"That'll be okay with me," Moore replied. "We can't take the whole crew in one trip anyway." Both men looked at the small thermal printer as it clattered to life, printing out the computer identification of the new arrival.

"Contact has changed course, Captain Patno," Kandar reported, "moving to course two-one-four. Speed increasing."

"Time to intercept?" Patno asked. Askart made a quick calculation.

"Twenty-five minutes to combat range," he answered.

"Make ready all tubes," Patno ordered. Askart relayed the message to the torpedo room.

"Tubes One through Eight ready, Captain," Askart reported a minute later.

"We will follow the new intruder," Patno explained, "if we are lucky, he will not hear us in his wake."

"Allah grant us luck, then," Askart whispered under his breath. He stepped close to Patno.

"Captain, may I speak to you in private?" Patno looked around, surprised that his executive officer would be so bold. The concerned look on Askart's face encouraged him to relent this once. He started for his cabin with Askart in tow.

Once inside the tiny cabin, Patno turned. "What is it?"

The executive officer looked pained, but answered immediately.

"Captain, that second contact can only be from one of three places, America, the Soviet Union, or France. There is little chance that there would be two British submarines in this area at the same time."

"Agreed," Patno replied, "what is your point?"

Askart looked surprised. "My point," he stammered, "is that if we attack a foreign vessel, we risk starting a war!"

The captain stood looking at Askart silently for a moment. "Lieutenant Askart," he said softly, "we are sailors. We do not start wars. Politicians start wars. We merely do the fighting and dying."

"But, Captain—" Askart protested.

"We have orders from President Mowati," Patno reminded the nervous officer. "Personally, I am more concerned with his response than I am with the Americans, the Russians, or the French. He does not look favorably upon disobedience."

The executive officer looked down at his feet for a moment, then looked Patno in the eye. "Forgive me for my impertinence, sir," he said firmly, "it was not my intention to question the president's orders." Patno smiled.

"Your concern is noted, Lieutenant, as is your loyalty," Patno answered. "Now let us get back to the problem at hand!"

"Distance to contact?" Gregoriy asked, leaning over the sonar operators.

"Six kilometers, Comrade Captain," Paolosky, the senior operator, answered. "Hull poppings and some machinery noise I cannot isolate."

The captain took a set of headphones and slipped them on, closing his eyes as he listened to the sound of the downed British submarine. He opened his eyes and fixed Paolosky with a stern look.

"You are sure this is the same contact?"

"He has not pinged again, Comrade Captain," the sonarman answered, "but this is the same submarine." The captain smiled and slipped the headset off, handing it to the junior operator. He turned to the intercom.

"Control Room, this is the captain," he began, "send up the VHF buoy and prepare to transmit." Ivask's voice crackled over the speaker.

"Just so, Comrade Captain," he replied, "buoy deployment commencing. Ready to transmit in eight minutes."

"Sonar," he admonished the two operators, "keep me informed of any changes in the contact."

"Exactly so!" the two enlisted men snapped as Gregoriy turned toward the radio console.

"Take this signal," he said to the radio operator, leaning close to keep the rest of the crew from overhearing. "Lost submarine located. On station six kilometers. Will await further instructions before making contact." He stood up and added, "Encrypt this for burst transmission."

"Just so, Comrade Captain," the radio operator answered. The captain turned to Ivask.

"Congratulations," the executive officer gushed, "this was very easy, in the event."

"Too easy," Gregoriy snapped, "besides, we have only found the boat. The salvage will be a bit harder."

"Indeed," Ivask agreed, "how long did it take the Americans to recover that sub of ours in the Pacific?"

The captain frowned. "Six years," he answered, "it sunk in 1968 and the Glomar Explorer raised part of the bow in 1974."

"But our navy has far more sophisticated equipment now!" Ivask insisted. The captain said nothing for a moment, arguing with himself about revealing the loss of the Pacific Fleet's only rescue submarine a few weeks before. There was little to tell, anyway. The sub's fate was still classified.

"That is true," he answered quietly. "We have plenty of time. The British have not built a new submarine class lately. Whatever we glean from this boat will still be operational."

"Comrade Captain," the radio operator called, "we are ready to transmit!"

"Do so!" the captain barked. The radio operator pressed the transmit key on his console, sending the message up the long wire to the buoy antenna tethered above them on the surface. The coded message, compressed into a high-speed "squeak," was repeated at ten-second intervals.

"Message sent!"

Gregoriy looked back over at Ivask. "Soon we will know how long we are to nursemaid this wreck," he speculated, "then we can go home."

"All tubes ready to fire, Captain," Askart reported. In front of him, the torpedo status lights glowed green.

"Flood all tubes and open outer doors," Patno ordered. A minute later two more rows of green lights glowed on the console.

"Ready, Captain," Askart said, his hand poised over the firing switches.

"At slow speed, fire One," Patno barked. Askart pressed the firing button. There was no perceptible indication that the torpedo had been fired.

The *19th of January*'s torpedoes "swam" out of their tubes without the aid of any compressed air or water pumps. That made their launch very quiet. The torpedoes had two speeds, a slow speed for searching and a faster attack speed. They swam out slowly, looking for their prey.

"One fired," he answered. A moment later he added, "Torpedo has locked on target. Switching to high speed and homing."

"Feed the data to Two and Three," Patno ordered. "Fire as soon as they are locked on target." The seconds dragged by as they waited for the torpedoes to digest the information fed to them by the one already closing with the target.

"Contact is evading," Kandar reported, studying his screen. "There is possibly a decoy in the water."

"Fire Two and Three!" Patno ordered. Askart flipped the firing switches.

"Two and Three away," he responded, "homing on target."

"New sonar contact!" Paolosky shouted. "Coming out of our baffle!"

"Identify!" the captain shouted. He turned back to Ivask. "I knew this was too easy!"

"Comrade Captain," the sonar operator called, "it is a diesel electric boat!" The sonar console's computer printer began to clatter.

"Diesel electric!" Gregoriy blurted. "Who has any diesel boats out here but us?"

"No one, Comrade Captain," Ivask answered. "The Americans and British have only nuclear boats. The French have diesel boats, but not in this ocean! It must be a local!"

"Local from where?" Gregoriy asked. "We're two hundred kilometers from any land."

Ivask was already searching the chart. "Manawatu, perhaps," he called, "it is the only nation with a fleet of any kind in this quadrant."

"Identification complete," the sonar operator called out, "German Type 209 submarine."

Gregoriy stepped over to the console and took the printout. On the rectangular sonar screen, a new series of thin lines appeared.

"Comrade Captain, he is flooding torpedo tubes!" Paolosky shouted, holding the headphones close to his head.

Gregoriy pressed the intercom button overhead. "Torpedo Room, flood tubes Three and Four! Open outer doors!" A chorus of "aye, ayes" answered him over the speaker. "Ivask, plot a solution to that boat and lock it in. Fire when locked!"

"Just so!" Ivask answered.

"Who is this maniac?" Gregoriy asked himself.

"Contact opening outer doors!" Paolosky shouted, his voice cracking with tension.

"Engine Room," the captain barked into the intercom, "emergency flank speed!" He turned to the helmsman. "Hard right rudder, thirty degrees down on the planes!"

The *Ulan Bator* heeled over to the right, her nose dropping as her captain tried desperately to pick up some speed and put as much distance as possible between his boat and the mysterious attacker. The hull groaned and popped under the sudden strain.

"High speed screws!" Paolosky screamed. "Torpedo in acquisition!"

"Has it locked on us?" Gregoriy shouted.

"Not yet!"

"Fire countermeasures when it locks!" Gregoriy shouted at the seaman on the fire control panel. The young sailor was too scared to answer. His eyes were wide with fear but he nodded vigorously.

"Answer up, Fire Control," Gregoriy snapped, "we are not sunk yet."

The young sailor found his voice. "Countermeasures ready, Comrade Captain!"

"Torpedo homing!"

"Fire the Nixie! Fire the countermeasures!" Gregoriy barked. "Where is that solution, Ivask?"

"Solution complete, locking in now!" Ivask called.

"Nixie and countermeasures fired!"

"Time to torpedo impact?" Gregoriy asked.

"Twelve seconds!" Paolosky answered. "More torpedoes in the water!"

"Tubes Three and Four ready!" Ivask shouted.

"Fire, dammit, fire!" Gregoriy shouted. Ivask pressed the two lighted buttons on the fire control panel. The sub shook as the two antisubmarine homing torpedoes blasted from their tubes.

"Reload Three and Four!" Gregoriy snapped. If the torpedoes homing in on them hit the *Ulan Bator,* reloading the tubes would be unnecessary. If the Nixie managed to draw them away, they might still win this fight.

Paolosky's voice broke into his frantic planning. "Impact in five, four, three." The sonarmen snatched off their headsets. "Two, one—"

The *Ulan Bator* seemed to jump forward. Gregoriy was thrown forward, barely able to catch himself on the helmsman's chair. Ivask and the fire control technician were both thrown to the deck. The others, strapped into their chairs, managed to remain at their stations.

Alarm bells of all sorts were ringing wildly. The control room was plunged into darkness as acrid smoke billowed from the air vents.

Gregoriy clawed his way up the chair to his feet as the dark red emergency lights came on.

"Damage reports!" he shouted into the intercom, trying to keep a grip on himself. Ivask climbed up over the unconscious body of the fire control technician and plugged his phones back in.

"Torpedo hit, starboard side engineering spaces," Ivask reported. "Taking water in the engine room and crew space." The smoke was getting thicker now. The sub, already heeled over in the turn, was listing steeply to starboard.

"Our torpedoes," Gregoriy snapped, "where are they?"

"Number Three is still running," Ivask shouted. "Four has lost its guidance wires."

"Has Three acquired yet?"

"No, Captain," Ivask responded, "it is still seeking."

"Find him, Vasili," the captain urged, then whispered under his breath, "or we are dead men!"

"Comrade Captain," the intercom squawked, "Engine Room. We are losing power on the batteries! We are unable to stop the water leaks!"

"Blow all tanks!" Gregoriy ordered. "Take us up. Emergency surface."

"Comrade Captain," Paolosky shouted, "two more torpedoes homing!"

"Time?"

"Ten seconds to impact!"

"Fire additional countermeasures!"

Ivask's hand went to the red switch again. Beneath the *Ulan Bator,* two more canisters shot away from the hull. Three seconds later they began to spew a cloud of metal flakes, hoping to lure the oncoming torpedoes.

"Torpedo deflecting, Comrade Captain," Paolosky reported, "it is following the Nixie!"

"The other?" Gregoriy asked.

"Still homing!" The sonarman looked around at the captain, his face stretched tight with panic. "It has ignored the countermeasures!"

"Time to impact?"

"One second to the Nixie!" Paolosky answered. A dull boom reverberated through the hull.

"Time to us?" Gregoriy shouted.

"Now!" the sonarman screamed. Another huge explosion shook the *Ulan Bator.* The emergency lights went out as the cold Pacific water rushed through the huge hole that blew through the pressure hull just below the sail, flooding the command center as the *Ulan Bator* died.

"Captain," Reg Jefferies called, ripping the printout from the machine, "contact is a Soviet Kilo-class attack sub!"

"What?" Jefferies ignored the question, listening intently to his phones.

"Active pinging, sir!" he shouted, then suddenly grew quiet, listening to the headphones. He looked up with a look of concern on his face. "He's searching!"

"I don't like this!" O'Connor cautioned.

"Neither do I!" Merganthal answered. He stepped over to the weapons console. "Do we have any weapons left working?"

"Negative, sir," O'Connor replied nervously, "torpedo room is flooded up to the top tubes."

"Damn!" Merganthal swore. "I hope that Soviet is here to rescue us, but I wouldn't bet on it!" He turned to Bob Moore. "Mr. Moore, I suggest that you take your little sub off a ways. These Russian fellows may not be humanitarians."

"I know all about Russian fellows," Moore answered, an enigmatic smile on his face. "How 'bout if I take some of the wounded with me?"

"Not just yet, I think," Merganthal demurred, "until we find out—"

"Captain," Jefferies shouted, "new contact! He's behind the Russian and opening his outer doors!"

"God in heaven!" Merganthal blurted, stepping across the control room to look over the sonarman's shoulder. "Who is he?"

"Unknown, Captain," Jefferies said quietly, "I'll see if the computer is still on-line." The sonarman punched a row of buttons on his console. A few seconds later the little printer rattled again. Jefferies tore off the strip of paper.

"What the—" he stammered.

"What is it, man?" Merganthal shouted.

Jefferies snapped his head around. "It's a German Type 209 submarine, sir!" he said, his voice tight with confusion. He offered up the printout. As Merganthal took it, Jefferies clasped his hands to his headphones again.

"Torpedo in the water!" he snapped. "Homing!"

"On us?" O'Connor asked.

"No, sir," Jefferies answered, "on the Russian! Two more torpedoes!"

A dull boom reverberated through the hull.

"Hit! The Russian is still under way! He's fired a Nixie!"

"Too late," O'Connor observed.

The sonarman looked up at the worried control room crew. "Torpedoes still homing. He doesn't have a prayer. Wait a minute—the Russian has fired two torpedoes!" A long moment passed.

"High speed propellors!" Kandar shouted. "Contact has fired one, no, two torpedoes."

Patno was about to order evasive action when a loud boom echoed through the hull.

"Torpedo One has hit!" the sonarman shouted again, wincing from the pain that shot through his ears.

"Where are his torpedoes?" Patno barked.

Kandar pressed his phones to his head as he stared at the shimmering lines on his scope.

"One torpedo is seeking," he blurted. "The other has lost lock and is running to starboard."

"Eject our countermeasures!" Patno snapped. Askart flipped up the protective cover over a recessed red button and pressed it.

"Countermeasures fired."

"Take us down," the captain said to the helmsman. The burly sailor nodded and pushed forward on the airplane-type yoke. The *19th of January* tipped forward as it dropped through the dark water.

"Countermeasure cloud has dispersed," Askart reported. "Our torpedoes have locked and are homing. It's just a matter of seconds now, Captain."

"For both of us, Number One," Patno observed.

"Enemy torpedo deflecting!" the sonarman shouted. "It's tracking the cloud!" The Soviet torpedo had been fooled by the billowing cloud of metal particles dispersed overhead by the countermeasures containers.

"Time on our torpedoes?" Patno asked quietly.

"Six seconds to impact," Kandar reported, "enemy is still maneuvering, but speed is slowing."

"We've got him!" Askart blurted. The captain remained silent, listening.

"Three, two, one—" Kandar counted down. Two distinct booms echoed through the hull. "Torpedoes Two and Three hit, Captain," the smiling sonarman exclaimed. "Their torpedoes have penetrated the cloud and lost lock."

"They may come back," Patno assured the man, "continue to track them. What is the enemy's condition?"

The sonarman was silent for a moment, then switched the set to loudspeaker. The command center was suddenly filled with metallic groans, pops, and a grinding sound that made everyone's skin crawl.

"Breaking up, Captain," Askart observed, "you got him!"

The captain was silent, his expression unreadable.

Sixty men dead in that Russian, Patno thought to himself, over a hundred in the English boat. How many, he wondered, how many more of us will die underwater today?

"Mr. Askart," he said briskly, "set course for the eye of the storm. We will report this engagement to base."

Askart stood watching until the captain disappeared into the companionway. He then turned to the helmsman.

"Helm, come back to zero-four-five," he ordered. "Close all outer doors, secure all weapons. Full speed ahead. Secure from action stations."

How strange, Askart thought as the crew went about their tasks, our first engagement, our first kill. How odd that Patno seems saddened by it.

He smiled slyly. Mowati would not be saddened! There would be promotions all around when they returned to Manawatu!

The sonarman's shout interrupted his dreams of glory.

"Torpedo in acquisition!" Kandar shot the two officers a glance. "It's one of the Russian's! It circled and found us!"

"Emergency speed!" Patno shouted. "Full blow! Take us up!"

The *19th of January* lunged forward as her five-bladed propellor bit into the cold water. The deck began to tilt as the sub ran for the surface.

"Do we have countermeasures left?" Patno called out as he returned to the attack center.

"One left, sir!" Askart answered.

"Fire it now!"

Askart again pressed the red switch to eject the canister of metal slivers.

The high-pitched pinging of the torpedo's active sonar rang softly through the sub, the interval between the incoming ping and the echo becoming shorter.

Patno and Askart watched the speed indicator as it climbed toward the Type 209's maximum twenty-two knots. That speed was less than half the speed of the Russian torpedo.

"The torpedo is approaching the countermeasure cloud!" Kandar called.

"Hard right rudder!" Patno called. He would try to evade the torpedo while its sonar was confused by the cloud of metal.

The *19th of January* banked into the turn, still racing for the surface. Behind it, the Soviet torpedo blew through the countermeasure cloud, its computer-driven scanner seeking a more substantial sonar return. It found one almost instantly.

"Torpedo homing!" the sonarman screamed. The incoming and return pings were very close now.

"Captain, what do we do now?" Askart gasped.

"Emergency dive!" Patno shouted. The deck leveled off for a moment, then pitched downward as the sub started back down.

"If this does not work," Patno observed, "then we will try to die like men."

Behind them, the Soviet torpedo bore on. As it entered the sub's turbulent wake, the torpedo's proximity fuse sensed the submarine's bulk and detonated the warhead.

In the attack center, the shock from the blast slammed everyone backward. Patno and Askart fell, the captain trying unsuccessfully to catch himself on the helmsman's chair.

"Full blow!" Askart shouted above the crew's screams. "Blow everything! Take it up!"

The crew struggled to work the equipment, terror numbing their minds.

"Damage reports!" Patno shouted as he struggled to his feet.

A frightened voice answered from the control room.

"The propellor is destroyed!" the engineering officer answered. "There is water coming in the machinery spaces! We have power, but there is water coming in the battery spaces, too."

"Put some air in the leaking spaces!" Patno ordered. He turned to the helmsman. "What is our depth?"

"Fifty meters, sir," the man replied. "The angle on the boat is negative."

"The flooding will soon correct that," Patno observed. As compressed air hissed from the storage tanks to the sub's ballast tanks, the deck came back level.

"Torpedo Room," Patno barked into the intercom, "open each remaining loaded tube one at a time and fire the torpedo. Only one tube at a time!"

A trembling voice answered in the affirmative.

Patno looked at Askart, whose confused and terrified expression made the captain laugh.

"We do not need the weight of ten torpedoes," he explained. As Askart nodded, Patno turned to the helmsman.

"What is our depth, now?" he asked, looking over the man's shoulder at the red digital readout.

"Forty-nine meters!" the helmsman answered, his voice shaking.

Patno patted the man on the shoulder and turned back to his executive officer.

"They have not sunk us yet, Askart!" The intercom crackled. The torpedo room reported as the first of the remaining torpedoes swam from its tube.

Askart's breathing was rapid now, and Patno could see the panic building behind his wide eyes.

"Mr. Askart!" Patno snapped. "What is the weight of each of our torpedoes?"

Askart stared at the captain, trying to focus his mind on the question.

"Did you hear me?" Patno snapped again. "What does a torpedo weigh?"

Askart blinked several times, fighting to remember.

"One thousand four hundred fourteen kilos, Captain," he stammered.

"Excellent!" Patno smiled. "How much weight will we save by firing the remaining torpedoes?"

Askart bent over the navigation table, using the small calculator fixed to the tabletop.

"Fifteen thousand five hundred fifty-four kilos," he answered, his voice calmer and the wild look fading from his eyes.

"Passing thirty meters!" the helmsman interrupted. The voice from the torpedo room crackled over the intercom again.

"Torpedo Five and Six away."

"Mr. Askart," the captain went on, "prepare a message for transmission. Report us as needing support. Do not send an SOS!"

Askart nodded and stepped over to the communications station to draft his radio message.

Patno patted the steel bulkhead and smiled.

"God bless the Germans," he murmured, "they know how to make submarines!"

Patno's face took on a somber look as he considered his own message to Mowati. The *19th of January* had accomplished its missions. It had located the downed submarine and defended it against an intruder. He would have to find a way to stress that success and minimize the damage to his own submarine. That would be tricky.

"Twenty meters!" the helmsman called. The intercom reported the emptying of the last torpedo tube. Patno reached over and pressed the switch.

"Reload all tubes and fire four of the reloads," he ordered. He would keep two tubes loaded. Better safe than sorry. If the extra weight became a problem, he could always fire them. For now, the problem was getting the sub to the surface and keeping it there. Almost as an afterthought, Patno remembered the storm.

10

Two booms, a few seconds apart, rang through the hull again.

"The Russian is dead, Captain," Jefferies reported. "Hull break-up noises and flooding coming from the Russian. No more noise from the 209."

"We're meat on the table for him, now!" O'Connor observed.

"I don't think so, Number One," Merganthal retorted, "I think he wants us alive."

"I hope you're right, Captain," Moore agreed.

"Sir, the 209 is closing his tubes," Jefferies reported, "he's not flooding anymore."

Merganthal and O'Connor exchanged distressed looks.

"Torpedoes," Jefferies said, staring intently at the scope. He turned back to the two officers. "The Russian's, sir. They're homing."

"Who are these bastards?" Merganthal wondered aloud.

"Dead ones," Jefferies offered. "One of those Russian fish has a lock on him."

The seconds dragged by as the dead Russian's torpedo bore down on his killer.

"Evasive actions," Jefferies reported. "He's blowing tanks."

Jefferies suddenly ripped the headphones away from his head as a boom echoed through the hull.

"Ivan got him, sir," Jefferies said.

"From the grave," O'Connor added.

Merganthal nodded. He turned to Bob Moore, who was standing next to the watertight door.

"Perhaps you should get under way as soon as possible, Mr. Moore."

"Looks like we're not so redundant after all," Moore observed.

"Indeed."

A touch on his sleeve caught Moore's attention.

"We have the worst of the wounded loaded, Bob," she said. "Who do you want to take the sub back? There's room for four more."

"I would like Mr. O'Connor to go with the wounded," Merganthal interrupted.

"Fine," Moore answered. "Carla, you, King, and Jackson take the sub back to the mine. You and King can stay with them and Tom can come back for the rest of us."

"On your way, Number One!" Merganthal ordered O'Connor.

O'Connor seemed confused for a second, then took one last look around the metal room that had been his duty station and home for so long.

"Aye, aye, Captain," O'Connor answered. He stepped over and shook Merganthal's hand. "Good luck, sir." O'Connor stepped back, executed a quick salute, and followed Carla aft to the waiting rescue sub.

As the two left, Moore looked at Merganthal.

"It looks like you've gotten yourself into the middle of a pissing contest, Captain!"

"I beg your pardon?" Merganthal asked, unsure of the expression.

"I mean," Moore explained, "it looks like there are folks out there that want your sub and are willing to fight and die for it."

"We'll see about that!" Merganthal answered.

• • •

"Damn this storm!" Khalil Chostsa muttered as another big wave broke over the bow of his coastal patrol boat. Behind Chostsa, a sailor gagged, fighting back the nausea that was inexorably taking over his crew.

They were good sailors, but this typhoon weather was enough to bring up even the hardest stomach. Chostsa had anticipated the rough seas and had a flat tin of Dramamine in his pocket. If worse came to worse, he would share it with the bridge crew.

Next to Chostsa, seemingly unaffected by the relentless motion, Malachi Fido sat looking out the circular, rain-splattered glass at the steel-gray sea, his feet braced against the chair's pedestal.

"How soon will we reach the area, Captain?" Fido asked again.

"One hour," Chostsa answered, "a little more if the storm worsens." Chostsa did not bother to share the knowledge that if the storm worsened, most of their small fleet would have to return to port. Fido would not hear it now. Better to let him see for himself later.

Through the side windows, Chostsa could see the other two patrol craft. They were wallowing as bad as his, trying to keep their headings.

Behind the three patrol boats, the *Star of Islam* plowed along. An old tramp steamer, she had been press-ganged into service. Her six large booms would haul up the precious cargo from the ocean floor. The thirty-year-old diving bell was lashed to her deck.

Another wave broke over the bow, the shock pitching each man against whatever structure he was using to keep upright. Behind him, Chostsa could hear the sailor lose his battle with mal de mer. The sickly sweet smell of vomit filled the bridge, bringing everyone's stomach into their throats. Only

Fido looked unaffected. He sat silently in his chair, a look of mild annoyance on his face.

Trying to ignore his protesting insides, Chostsa went over his orders again. Fido was in command of a—what? An expedition to bring up some "national treasures" from the seabed far offshore. Chostsa's boats and the requisitioned freighter were at his disposal.

Chostsa looked again at his chart, sealed up in a clear plastic envelope to keep it dry. The spot Fido had marked was devoid of any treasure Chostsa knew of. The whole area was a deep trench over the Voorman Fault, a volcanic area well out of their normal patrol routes.

"What are we looking for, Minister Fido?" Chostsa asked, using the title with hesitation. Fido did not turn, but cast a quick glance at him.

"For a sunken submarine. You have no need for more knowledge than that, Captain," he answered, "you only need to worry about getting us there and protecting us while we are there. Do not concern yourself with any other details."

"By your command," Chostsa replied, grasping a steel handhold as another wave broke over them. He would not ask again. It would only mean trouble. Besides, if the storm got any worse, it would be immaterial. In his heart, Chostsa prayed for a worsening storm. They could go home then, and put off this mission. Its suddenness and secrecy made him nervous, as did the presence of Malachi Fido. Where Fido went, weirdness and trouble always followed. It was doubtful that anything good would come of this little trip, especially for the crews of the four boats.

As the deck pitched again, Chostsa looked at his watch. The time was passing slowly, but he was in no hurry to get there.

• • •

Thomlinson, the last injured man into the little sub, was unconscious. His skull had cracked when his head had slammed into a steel control box in the engine room as the *Revenge* had crashed to the rocky ocean floor. The bleeding had stopped, but the man's pupils were different sizes now, a bad sign.

King and O'Connor followed Thomlinson up into the cramped sub. Below them, Bob Moore smiled, gave them a thumbs-up, and pulled down the *Revenge*'s hatch. King and O'Connor closed the minisub's hatch and dogged it tight.

"All set, Tom," King called as the locking lugs engaged the recesses in the sub's hull.

In the pilot's chair, Tom Jackson gave them a thumbs-up and flipped the switches on his console. Air whooshed into the space between the two submarines, breaking the pressure seal. A moment later the little sub rocked free of its large broken brother.

"Here we go, folks," Jackson called to the injured passengers. "Next stop: DeepCore mining outpost Rock Sucker."

A ragged, pained cheer rose from the back. The wounded men were happy to be off the downed sub, but worried about their shipmates back on *Revenge.*

"Soon as we drop you guys off," Jackson added to help quell their concern, "we'll be back for the rest! No problem!"

I shouldn't have said that, Jackson reprimanded himself, every time I say "no problem," there always is one. He pushed the sub's control sticks forward. The thrusters whirred, pushing the little sub toward its undersea home a hundred kilometers away.

As the huge dark bulk of the *Revenge* disappeared below, Jackson prayed that the wrecked sub and its occupants would be all right until he returned.

11

"Minister," Chostsa said, "we are over the spot now." Fido's eyes blinked open. He had actually fallen asleep! How he could doze when everyone around him was racked by seasickness was a mystery.

"Have you made contact with the *19th of January*?" Fido asked.

"Not yet," Chostsa answered, "we are hailing her now." Fido nodded and stood, stretching and stifling a yawn. Outside, the sea was still high, the boats pitching and rolling.

He mustn't have any human weakness, Chostsa thought, he doesn't even seem to notice. A sly smile crept across Chostsa's face.

Perhaps the man isn't human, he mused, maybe the rumors are true.

The radio speaker suddenly came to life, gargling and squawking a jumble of static-broken words. The ashen-faced radio operator turned to Chostsa.

"I think," he gasped, "I think it's the *19th of January*!"

"Captain," Askart urged, "we must submerge deeper!" The captain, holding the radio operator's headset to his ear, ignored the request.

Askart tried again. "Captain, we are taking more water in the engineering spaces! The storm is shaking us to pieces!"

Patno held up his hand for silence. A smile of relief flashed across his face.

"Take us down to thirty-five meters, Mr. Askart," Patno ordered. Askart nodded to the helmsman, who pushed the yoke forward with obvious relief.

"The fleet, such as it is, has found us," Patno reported as the *19th of January* slowly slipped beneath the storm's reach. "Were we able to recharge the batteries?"

"To some extent, Captain," Askart answered. "Some are damaged. We have enough battery power for several hours, if no other problems arise."

"Hopefully, we will be able to surface soon and get back to port," Patno said.

"I hope so, Captain," Askart agreed, "we could not survive the storm on the surface."

"While we are waiting," Patno suggested, "get the men into their survival gear and get the rafts ready in case we have to abandon the boat."

"Pray God we do not have to!" Askart answered.

"Comrade Fleet Admiral," the young Signal captain solemnly reported, "the *Ulan Bator* does not respond to either blue-green laser or Extra Long Frequency transmissions."

Ganilev did not answer but sat staring at his subordinate. The unwavering gaze made the captain nervous. Obviously, the admiral wanted to know more than just the bad news.

"We are, of course, continuing to transmit by both mediums," the captain went on, "as well as by coded VHF radio. If she is out there and able to transmit, we will hear her."

The admiral got up from the plush red leather chair and turned to the windows that faced the wide square next to the building.

"Is it possible that the storm has interfered with their transmission?" Ganilev asked, not looking around.

"It is indeed possible," the captain answered, searching for some reason other than the worst case, "however, the ELF transmission is not affected by weather. The *Ulan Bator* would have received the status request several times by now."

The admiral was silent for a moment, then turned and pressed the intercom switch. "Have the chief of Naval Intelligence report to my office immediately," he said softly. This done, he looked up at Borskov's worried face.

"Thank you, Signal Captain," Ganilev said, dismissing the officer, "keep me informed of your progress."

"Just so, Comrade Fleet Admiral!" Borskov answered, saluting the admiral's back as he turned again to the windows.

He was still looking out the window when Elias Marshak, his top intelligence officer, knocked softly on the office door, walked to the desk, and saluted.

Ganilev looked around at Marshak, who stood casually, waiting for his commander's questions. Marshak, formerly an Olympic gymnast, was shorter than most of his fellow officers, but far more canny and intelligent. He had risen through the ranks rapidly after a knee injury ended his athletic career.

"What naval assets capable of engaging our submarine exist in the target area?" Ganilev asked, avoiding the more serious expression "capable of sinking."

Marshak was ready for the question. Since the *Ulan Bator* had been ordered into the area, Marshak had studied every bit of naval data available about the region.

"Comrade Fleet Admiral," he began, "there is only one local force capable of even finding the *Ulan Bator*. That is the small Manawatuan navy." Marshak produced a small map and spread it on Ganilev's desk. The admiral bent slightly to examine it.

"Manawatu has four Chinese coastal patrol craft, none of which is equipped with sonar sophisticated enough to find the *Ulan Bator* in deep water," Marshak went on. "They have a squadron of jet fighters bought from the French and a pair of Pucara propellor aircraft purchased from the Argentines."

"Skip their inventory, Marshak," Ganilev growled, "tell me what I asked for."

"Exactly so, Comrade Fleet Admiral," Marshak continued, unperturbed. "Although they took great pains to conceal its purchase, we know that Manawatu has a single German Type 209 submarine, which they purchased at great expense from the Indonesians." Marshak was gratified to see his information have such an effect on his commander. Ganilev was listening closely now, his brows knit together like a gray cloud bank over his watery blue eyes.

"The purchase included crew training and twenty-five German SUT torpedoes," Marshak explained. "We believe they have expended four or five of those torpedoes in training. Of the others, fourteen are carried as a normal load on the Type 209."

"This Type 209 has the range to reach the target area?" Ganilev asked.

"Easily," Marshak answered. "It also has sufficient sonar and combat control equipment to successfully engage another submarine, such as the *Ulan Bator,* but to do so would require a skilled submarine commander and we know of no such person in their navy."

Ganilev was silent for a moment. "Tell me about Manawatu," he asked, easing himself back into the big chair and gesturing Marshak to sit in the single hardback chair that faced his desk.

"Manawatu is a confederation of small islands," he began. "The ruler, one Sendu Mowati, is an unstable egomaniac who rules the islands with an iron fist and a soft brain."

"A familiar type," Ganilev snorted.

"Indeed," Marshak agreed. "We, I mean the Soviet Union, once courted him as a possible ally in the region. It was decided that there was little to be gained by that alliance and only low-level diplomatic relations exist now." Marshak chuckled. "A posting to Manawatu is considered a punishment tour in the intelligence corps," he added.

"It would seem that this Mowati is not the addled moron you have depicted to me," Ganilev countered. "We cannot make contact with the *Ulan Bator* and now you tell me that this island maniac has an attack submarine!"

Marshak was silent. His intelligence section had given slight credence to Manawatu's submarine threat. After all, one could not expect a group of monkeys to produce *War and Peace* simply because they possessed a typewriter.

The admiral was silent, staring at the map of Manawatu. Finally, he looked up and the expression on his face was unsettling.

"In one hour, I want you to brief the chief of operations on Manawatu's entire military posture," he ordered. "Please do not omit anything from this briefing."

"In no way!" Marshak answered, standing. Ganilev turned the chair toward the windows. At his gesture of dismissal, Marshak saluted and left the office.

Ganilev turned and again pressed the intercom button. "Have the chief of operations and his planning staff meet me in the plans room in an hour," he instructed his aide. He released the button in the middle of the aide's affirmative answer. He looked up at the framed photo of Sergei Georgiyevich Gorshkov, the first admiral of the Fleet of the Soviet Union, the father of the modern Soviet Navy.

"Once again," Ganilev told the picture of Gorshkov, "a piss-ant seeks to do battle with giants."

An hour later Ganilev walked into the plans room in the subbasement of his headquarters. Buried deep below the surface and surrounded by thick reinforced concrete, the plans room was the heart of the Pacific Fleet's operations.

Waiting for him were Vice-Admiral Pyotr Petrovich, the chief of operations, and his senior planning staff.

"Keep your seat, comrades," Ganilev snapped as the assembled officers rose. Ganilev walked to the head of the table and sat in the big chair there. He scanned the faces seated around the table until he found Borskov.

"Is there any communication from the *Ulan Bator*?" he asked.

"None, Comrade Fleet Admiral," the Signal officer replied. Ganilev frowned.

"Admiral Petrovich," Ganilev went on, nodding to his old friend, "it seems that our submarine searching for the downed British missile submarine has either developed radio trouble or been lost." The men around the table exchanged nervous glances.

A submarine lost from an onboard accident or communication trouble would mean a simple search and rescue operation. A submarine sunk by hostile action was another matter. The planning team was still smarting from the failure of the mission to steal the Americans' submarine tracking system a few weeks before.

"Comrade Colonel Marshak will brief you on the possible threats in the area," Ganilev said, nodding toward Marshak. The GRU officer stood and scanned the faces watching him.

"Comrade Fleet Admiral," he began, nodding at Ganilev, "Comrade Admiral, the area in which we believe the British ballistic missile submarine *Revenge* has gone down is near the island nation of Manawatu." Marshak nodded to his aide, who placed a large map of the area on an easel.

"Manawatu has a small surface fleet that offers little threat to a modern submarine," Marshak went on, "but we believe that they have one German Type 209 submarine that they secretly purchased from the Indonesians." The aide placed an illustration of a Type 209 on the easel.

"The Type 209 is a very capable boat," Marshak explained, "however, we question whether they have a skilled crew and captain to man it." Eyebrows went up around the table.

"In the event that they do have a good crew," Marshak speculated, "they might well have been able to successfully engage the *Ulan Bator*."

"What purpose would that serve?" Admiral Petrovich asked.

"If Manawatu could recover any or all of the British nuclear weapons," Marshak explained, "they would be in a position to blackmail both the South Pacific and Southeast Asian regions."

"As well as the other nations who have an interest in the region?" Petrovich interrupted.

"Exactly!" Marshak answered.

"One would think that these petty little despots would learn from the fate of others of their ilk," Ganilev observed. "That fool Hussein threatened to use atomic weapons after he seized Kuwait! That threat did not save him."

There were chuckles and nods of agreement around the table.

"This fool doesn't even have any delivery vehicles capable of reaching even his nearest neighbors!" Marshak went on. "It is unclear to what end he would desire to obtain such weapons. Nevertheless, he must be considered a threat."

"What possibility is there that the Mayday message was a trick to lure us into a trap of some sort?" Petrovich asked.

"There is certainly that possibility," Marshak agreed, "however, there would be no way to forecast who would respond to such a trick, nor any plausible motivation."

"Who can read these monkeys' motivations?" Petrovich asked rhetorically.

"Thank you, comrade," Ganilev interrupted, cutting short Petrovich's speculation. "Admiral Petrovich, I want you to assign one of our cruise missile submarines to find the *Ulan Bator* and the British submarine, if indeed it is really there." Ganilev looked at the tabletop for a moment and added a more serious addendum to the order.

"If you determine that the *Ulan Bator* has been sunk by hostile action," he said slowly, "prepare your missiles for launching at the attacker!"

This order took everyone by surprise. The nuclear-tipped cruise missiles had never been fired in anger.

As the others filed out of the room, Petrovich remained behind.

"Comrade Fleet Admiral," he began, "it will require an order of the Supreme Soviet to fire the missiles. I cannot order a submarine commander to violate his standing orders."

Ganilev fixed his operations chief with a placid stare. The man was only pointing out the obvious to him. That was part of his duties.

"The South Pacific is a big place, Comrade Admiral," Ganilev responded, "there are few satellites to watch and fewer observers. If we have to chasten this little pirate, no one will be too distressed." He smiled at his subordinate's discomfort.

"Besides," he went on, "it will be hard to prove who fired the missiles after they detonate!"

"Just so," Petrovich agreed, the nervousness barely disguised in his voice.

12

The soft knock woke Mikhail Vortmet.

"Come," he coughed.

Senior Lieutenant Valentin Somolov, the executive officer, stuck his head into Vortmet's cabin. "Sorry to wake you, Comrade Captain, but we have a signal from Pacific Fleet."

Vortmet sat up, yawned, and ground the sleep from his eyes with his knuckles. He stuck his hand out and Somolov put the printed message into it.

Vortmet read the message, his eyes growing wide. He looked up at Somolov, suddenly awake.

"Did you ask for confirmation of this?"

"Not yet, Comrade Captain," Somolov answered, "I wanted you to see it first."

"Ask for confirmation," Vortmet said. He stood and turned to the small basin as Somolov disappeared.

Await firing orders, he mused. In the three years he had commanded the *Omsk*, he had never gotten an order to fire. He had assumed that he never would. Of his twenty-four SS-N-19 cruise missiles, eighteen had thousand-kilo conventional high-explosive warheads. The remaining six were tipped with 350-kiloton nuclear warheads. His submarine had the power of a Kirov-class surface cruiser.

He and his crew had fired conventionally tipped SS-N-19s in practice. To his knowledge, no one had fired a nuclear one.

He glanced at his watch. At thirty-five knots submerged, the *Omsk* would be on station in twenty-two hours.

It would be prudent, he thought as he dried his face, to see what is within 450 kilometers of that spot. Then, at least, he would have an idea who he might have to kill.

In the wide command center, Somolov was waiting.

"I have asked for confirmation, Comrade Captain," he reported. "We are at full speed and I have set course for the designated area." Vortmet smiled.

"I could have stayed in bed," he said brightly, "you have everything under control!"

Somolov's face betrayed no emotion. It was no secret that he coveted a command of his own.

"Forgive me for anticipating your orders, Comrade Captain."

"Not at all, Somolov." Vortmet laughed, stepping over behind the diving station to check the sub's depth and course.

A signalman stepped through the hatch. Somolov took the offered message.

"Fleet has confirmed the order, Comrade Captain," he said, passing the message to Vortmet.

"Very well, comrade," Vortmet answered, "bring the charts of the area and have the officers meet me in the wardroom."

"Minister," Chostsa reported, "we have made contact with our submarine."

"And?" Fido asked.

"They are heavily damaged, Minister," Chostsa answered. "They engaged a Soviet submarine and sunk it, but *19th of January* suffered a torpedo hit. They have no power." Fido frowned. That was not the answer he was seeking.

"Why have they not made contact?" he asked.

"They were too heavily damaged to surface in these high seas, Minister," Chostsa replied. "We made contact with them by lowering an antenna."

Seeing his worsening scowl, Chostsa disappeared down the stairs to the tiny radio room. Fido looked out the rain-soaked glass at the heaving gray sea.

Either the storm is abating, he thought, or I am getting used to it. The patrol boat did not seem to be pitching as violently now.

The damaged sub could not help him locate the Englishman. Or could it? Fido unbuckled himself from the chair and made his lurching way down the stairs after Chostsa.

In the tiny radio room, Chostsa was on the horn to the submarine captain. Fido stepped up and took the microphone from Chostsa.

"This is Malachi Fido," he barked into the handset, "who am I speaking to?"

There was a brief pause, then a badly distorted voice came over the speaker.

"Captain Patno here, Minister."

"Patno," Fido asked, "what is your status? Are you sinking?"

After another slight pause, Patno answered.

"No, Minister," he said cautiously, "we are in no immediate danger, but we have no power."

"Is your sonar operable?" Fido asked.

"It is, Minister, although our battery power is down and we cannot maneuver. We request a tow back to our dock."

"Request denied!" Fido snapped. "Your country requires your service here." The others in the room, Chostsa, the radio operator, and a leathery-looking old petty officer, exchanged a brief disbelieving look, taking care to wipe their faces free of any expression before Fido could see.

"Did you get a fix on the downed British submarine before the Russian appeared?" Fido continued his interrogation.

"No, Minister," the wavering voice answered, "we were

engaged in combat before we could locate it. The Russian may have found it, though."

"Why do you think that?"

"He was pinging heavily in the area, and there was possibly another sonar operating as well."

Fido looked around the small radio room, digesting this last information. The room was all metal, including the thin desk and chair in front of the radios, which were stacked against the forward bulkhead. The petty officer and Chostsa had backed out of the room to give him space to move around.

Another sonar. Surely the Englishman wasn't still alive. Fido rolled his eyes. It was possible. The *19th of January* was still alive after a torpedo hit. Maybe the Englishman was, too. That made it more complicated. If it had sonar, it might have weapons, as well.

"Captain Patno," Fido said, his voice softer now, "what weapons would an English nuclear missile submarine carry?"

There was a long pause. Fido was about to repeat his question when Patno came back on the line.

"Minister," he answered, "in addition to his sixteen missiles, he would carry eighteen Mk 24 Tigerfish torpedoes in six bow tubes."

"What is your weapons status?" Fido asked.

Again there was a long pause. "We have two torpedoes remaining, Minister." There seemed to be something in Patno's voice that Fido could not identify, but it did not matter.

"Captain," Fido said loudly for the benefit of those standing behind him outside the radio room, "prepare to receive a towline. We will use your sonar to locate the Englishman. When that is accomplished, your submarine will be towed to port."

"Yes, Minister," Patno responded quickly, then added, "we

cannot stay submerged indefinitely. We will need to surface for air in a few hours."

"When that time comes, we will make arrangements, Captain," Fido assured the man, "until then, you have your orders."

Fido handed the microphone back to the impassive radioman and went back up to the bridge.

Perhaps, he speculated on the way up the stairs, the need for air will spur him to find the Englishman faster.

"This is insane!" Askart shouted. "We cannot continue our mission! We are lucky to be alive now!"

"I agree," Patno answered, "but I am not in the mood to tell Malachi Fido that I will not do as he bids." Around the command center, there were nods of agreement. Fido's reputation was almost legend.

Patno put his hand on Askart's shoulder. "I have known people who resisted the man's will," he assured his nervous exec, "they always seemed to vanish, along with their families." He looked around at the others. "If something happens to us, at least our families will not suffer." Askart looked back with a pained expression.

"Besides," Patno went on, "we fought the Russian and survived! Surely we can survive our own navy, too!"

Patno leaned close to Askart's ear. "Besides, we still have two tubes loaded. We will survive this, Askart, and be welcomed home as heroes."

The executive officer did not look reassured.

"Are we going to make it?" Carla asked, peering over Jackson's shoulder at the small cluster of dials on the console just in front of his right shoulder.

"Yeah, I think so"—he grinned back at her—"I'd hate to have to paddle this tub!"

"Really."

"How're our passengers?" he asked.

"A couple of 'em look bad," she whispered. "I don't know if they'll make it to the mine. The others are hanging in there."

"We were in such a rush to leave the mine," he complained, "I forgot to do something."

"What?" she asked.

"I forgot to switch the radio over to repeater mode, so we could call home from out here. Now we'll just have to wait till we get there to call DeepCore."

Carla laughed. "I switched it over when I went to pee," she said. "That's what took me so long!"

"It's not fair, Carla," Jackson complained, "it really isn't!"

"What?"

"You're so smart and so good-looking," he whined, "and all I got was this huge reproductive organ."

"Hey," she cooed, patting his shoulder, "there's just no justice!"

Jackson chuckled and handed her the radio headset over his shoulder. "Why don't you see if you can reach DeepCore," he suggested. "If you can't, we'll try again every five minutes until someone answers."

Carla slipped on the headset and slid her arm past Jackson to press the transmit button on the radio console.

"DeepCore," she called, "this is Rock Sucker, over." She waited impassively for a moment, then repeated the message.

"Nothing," she said, slipping off the headset, "I'll give 'em another shout in a few minutes."

Jackson nodded as she returned to tending the wounded. He scanned the gauges. They had enough power to get back to the mine—if nothing happened and if his navigation was right on.

He silently blessed Carla for turning on the repeater. Even if they got lost, they could still holler for help.

The air was hot and so fetid that he was almost asleep when he heard the first metallic pop. That was followed by something high-pitched that sounded like screaming. Engine noise drowned out the high-pitched sound. Another pop followed, then another.

"Captain, I'm picking up all sorts of weird noises topside," Jefferies called.

"How weird, Jefferies?" Merganthal asked, picking up the extra headphone and pressing it to his ears.

Merganthal listened for a while, then put down the headset.

"What do you make of it?" he asked Jefferies.

"Engine noise, several power plants," Jefferies said, "I think that popping is a towline!" He swiveled in his seat to face the captain. "I heard something like it a couple of years ago when Ivan had a problem with one of his old November-class boats off the Azores. We trailed him a ways and listened to his rescue party when they towed him in. It sounded just like that!"

"Who the hell is towing whom?" Merganthal wondered aloud.

"I imagine that that Type 209 is getting some help from his Manawatuan buddies," Bob Moore interrupted. He tapped the chart on the navigation table as Merganthal came over. "Unless I'm mistaken, the only place close enough to get someone here to help him this fast is the Republic of Manawatu."

Merganthal looked at the chart and whistled. "And ruled by a jumped-up little lunatic named Mowati," Merganthal added. "Well, that's wonderful, isn't it?"

"Wonder if it was him that set those mines for you?"

"I doubt that very much," Merganthal answered. "It would be nearly impossible to guess our exact route or the effect of the storm." He snorted. "Besides, if we even thought for a second that he ambushed us, we have the power to vaporize his pip-squeak republic."

"Well, whether he planned it or not," Moore went on, "it looks like he's taking advantage of the situation." Moore hooked his thumb aft. "I suspect he wants those warheads you're carrying."

"You must be daft," Merganthal answered. "What could he do with them? He doesn't have the means to use them!"

"Really?" Moore countered. "He's got jet aircraft, boats, and at least one submarine. Besides, he can always sell a couple to other folks who'll trade the tools to deliver them for the warheads."

Merganthal didn't answer, but returned to Jefferies's sonar station. "What are our new neighbors doing now, Jefferies?"

"Hard to say for certain, Captain," the sonarman answered. "There's still lots of screw noise, but it's not going away." Jefferies looked up at his captain. "If anything, it's circling!"

"This is insane," Merganthal complained. "Here we are, one of the most powerful vessels that ever sailed, and we're caught like rats in a trap!"

"Captain Patno," Askart hissed as the *19th of January* lurched again, "this pounding will tear us apart! We cannot go on like this any longer!"

Indeed, each surge of the thick steel towline produced a new series of groans and pops from the already damaged hull.

"Your concern is noted, Mr. Askart," Patno replied, "but we have no say in the matter." A wave of incredulity swept over Askart's face. Around them, the other crew obviously shared Askart's fear.

"I suggest that you make sure each man has his emergency gear on and that the escape hatch is in working order," Patno ordered. "Hopefully, we will not have to endure the towing much longer."

"It's not the towing," Askart emphasized, "it's the direction! He's towing us back to the battle area, not to our base!"

"That is not our decision," Patno reiterated. "We are following orders here!"

"Following them to our deaths," Askart whispered.

"If need be, Mr. Askart," Patno stressed, "if need be." He turned to the sonar operator.

"Have you picked up any return from the British submarine?"

Kandar looked up, his face damp with sweat and tight with fear. "No, Captain, I have not." He looked uncertain for a second, then spoke up. "Captain, how will we be able to tell the English sub from the Russian one we sunk?"

"The English sub is three times the size of the Russian," Patno explained. "Besides, the Russian should still be giving off noise. The Englishman may not."

The operator nodded but did not seem reassured. Like the rest of the crew, he was scared.

They were so filled with their own courage when they were the hunters, Patno reflected, now they know how it feels to be the prey.

Despite Askart's dire warnings, Patno had faith in his boat. The Germans knew how to build strong ships. The *19th of January* was damaged, but it was still operational and in no immediate danger of sinking, storm or no storm. As long as they stayed submerged and didn't try to run on the surface, they would be all right.

The sub lunged again and one of the crew cried out in fear.

"Mr. Askart," Patno said loudly, "we will conduct a stand-down inspection in ten minutes and an emergency evacuation drill after that! Give the order now!"

Askart shook off his own fear and barked the order through the intercom. Slowly, as if they were coming awake from a coma, the crew began to respond.

If I can keep them thinking about something else, Patno mused, or make them fear failure more than death, we may, Inshallah, come through this.

13

Ismet Palatin clutched the cold steel rail and vomited hard over the edge. The spray from a breaking wave blew much of the puke back in his face, nauseating him even more. His guts twisted, bending him over the rail, and for one terrifying second, Ismet thought he was going over.

He locked his feet under the rail's bottom rung and twisted his foot against the upright, wedging him into the railing. It was stupid to be here in the first place, but even more stupid to die out here on this fool's errand.

Between waves of nausea, Ismet watched the two patrol craft towing the damaged submarine.

Oh, to be down there with them! Ismet prayed. Under the waves, it was calm. Better to be on a damaged submarine than riding this wallowing freighter!

The horizon tilted again and Ismet's stomach rose up to meet it.

"This mission is insane," he gagged. "Our leader is insane and I am insane!" His face twisted in imitation of his tortured innards as he clutched the rail and prayed to die.

This was the price of pride, he told himself, squeezing his eyes shut tight to keep out the wild sea spray. He had been so proud to work with the Americans when they came to explore the void that lay beyond Manawatu's long barrier reef. They had trained him to work the diving bell and he had accompanied them on dozens of descents in the round bell as they photographed the denizens of the deep and mapped the abyss. He had been a hero to his friends and had even received a bronze plaque from the Americans when they left Manawatu.

The plaque hung in his home, now. It had been his ticket here.

Once an object of pride, the plaque was a plague to him now, the words "*National Geographic* Magazine" a curse. His stomach twisted again, but there was nothing to throw up. The bitter, awful taste of bile filled his mouth. He retched, crying out to God for mercy.

A snapping sound behind him caught his attention. Palatin looked around just in time to see the big metal ratchet on the end of one of the nylon straps that held the diving bell to the deck fly up and hit him.

The blow stunned him. There was no pain, really, just a numbness on the left side of his head. He squeezed his eyelids tight and tried to shake his head, to shake off the numbness. When he moved his head, the pain came. Ismet opened his mouth to yell, but no sound came out.

Black lace curtains seemed to be closing over his vision and he fought to keep them open. On the deck, the diving bell was sliding away from him as the ship rolled to starboard. Ismet watched as it slid into the rail, bending the railing out over the side of the ship.

The bell, strapped to a huge pallet, tipped and for a moment Ismet thought it would fall over the side. He prayed it would. If the bell disappeared, the mission was over.

He moaned in pain and disappointment as the bell hung motionless for a second, then righted itself and dropped back onto the deck, which now began to tilt to port. In a terrifying flash, Ismet realized that the bell would soon be on its way to him.

He struggled to free his wedged foot from the railing, but his arms and legs seemed to belong to someone else. The black curtains were drawing closed. He knew that the bell would begin its slide toward him any second and knew that this time it would not be stopped by the thin rail.

He and it would plunge into the steel-gray sea. He knew that he would be dead before he hit the water, cut into three large chunks as the bell ripped through the rail and fell into the Pacific. A sudden delirious vision of sharks ripping into big chunks of meat filled his mind.

He tried again to scream and failed. As the black lace closed over him, he heard voices on deck, shouting voices, frightened voices. Ismet tried to listen, tried to care about the shouted orders, but he could not.

The deck seemed to vibrate beneath him. A huge mass swept by in the darkness. Ismet felt it hit the rail beside him and braced for the pain. It never came.

Confused and suddenly very tired, Ismet slumped forward, trying to blot out the screaming voices that sought to keep him awake.

Plena Whitcox watched as first one, then the other restraining strap broke on the diving bell. The ratchet from one of the straps flew across the deck and hit the man clinging to the railing.

"Oh, please," Whitcox moaned, "not this!" He thumbed the intercom box to All Stations and shouted into it.

"All hands on deck!" he barked. "Shifting cargo on deck! All hands forward to secure cargo!"

He watched helplessly as the crew scrambled onto the pitching deck, headed for the loose bell. The bell was now caroming off the starboard rail. Whitcox held his breath as it tipped, hung motionless, then fell back on deck. His relief was short-lived. The ship pitched to port and the bell began to slide that way, straight for the man who clung to the rail.

The man was hanging on to the rail and weaving. Even from a distance, Whitcox could see blood on the man's head. The deck gang was running for the bell now, dragging chains with them to capture the runaway bell as it began its slide to port.

The two straps on the bell's starboard side held for a moment, stopping the bell in the center of the deck. Then the aft strap broke. The bell twisted toward the bow. The forward strap, stretched to the limit, broke, too. The bell was now free on deck, a loose cannon. It slid toward the port rail, but missed the slumped figure there. Slowed by the two straps, it caught on the rail and hung there. The crew swarmed over it, tossing chains to secure it to the rail. Others ran blocks across the deck, shackling them to the deck cleats. Once the bell was secured to the rail, they would try to haul it across to the center of the deck again.

Whitcox turned to the seaman behind him. The man was staring wide-eyed at the drama on deck.

"Get down there!" Whitcox shouted. "Tell them to use twice as much chain as they think they need! I don't want that bell loose again!"

The sailor disappeared down the ladder.

"A diving bell in a typhoon!" Whitcox muttered. "What a cracked idea!" He quickly looked around to see if anyone had overheard his complaint. Mowati had spies everywhere and all it took was one lapse to make a person disappear.

If my English ancestor could see me now, he thought, shaking his head, he would laugh in my face!

Whitcox's grandfather had come to Manawatu between the wars, looking for paradise. The old man had been lucky enough to die while it still was a paradise, before Mowati had taken power.

"You would be laughing at me, Grandfather, to see me now," Whitcox said ruefully, "I am laughing at myself."

Below, the crew had the bell pulled tight between two sets of blocks, pulling it slowly back to the center of the deck. The injured man was stumbling between two sailors as they took him toward the stairs that led below.

Whitcox said a quick prayer first to his grandfather's Christian God, then to Allah, then to Janu, the ancient God of the Sea.

When a man was engaged in stupidity like this, he decided, he couldn't get enough gods on his side.

"Minister," Chostsa reported, "the diving bell broke loose on the deck of the freighter. Captain Whitcox says it has been secured now, but the bell operator, a man named Palatin, was injured."

"Injured how badly?" Fido asked, never taking his eyes from the two patrol boats that were towing the damaged submarine ahead.

"He was hit on the head and has a concussion."

"No broken bones or internal injuries?" Fido asked, turning at last toward Chostsa.

"No, Minister."

"Was the bell damaged?"

"No, Minister."

Fido smiled and went back to staring out the streaked window. "Thank you, Captain," he said softly, "keep me advised."

Chostsa spoke briefly with the burly seaman at the wheel, then went back below. He was maintaining constant contact with the other captains, particularly the two who were towing the submarine. When Whitcox had called in about his accident, Chostsa had been disappointed that the bell had not fallen overboard. He had later realized that Fido would merely have stopped and found some way to recover the bell before going back after his real goal, the British submarine.

That missing submarine was all that mattered to him. If he had to sacrifice every vessel in this ragtag little fleet to find that sunken English sub, he would do it without a second thought.

Better to find the thing quickly and get what they could from it. That was the only way any of them would be going back.

Chostsa stepped into the cramped head and locked the door. He dug into the inside pocket of his foul-weather jacket and pulled out the thin, curved flask hidden there. Chostsa twisted off the plastic cap and took a long swig.

The fiery cognac burned its way down his throat, sending a tremor ahead of it the length of his body. Chostsa took a deep breath, then coughed on the strong alcohol fumes. He rinsed his mouth to hide the cognac smell on his breath. He did not know if Fido was a dedicated Moslem, like their ruler, but it did not pay to take chances with the man. Fortified by the strong drink, Chostsa left the head and went back upstairs.

Palatin woke up in the freighter's infirmary. At first, his eyes would not focus on the same spot, but in a few seconds, the twin images merged into the florid face of Dr. Bina, the ship's hastily recruited physician.

"So, you are still alive, eh?" Bina asked. "How do you feel?"

Ismet tried to raise his head. Pain like two sledgehammers hitting the side of his head simultaneously urged him to remain flat on his back and he quickly complied.

"Like my head has been used to drive pilings!" Ismet answered weakly. Bina chuckled.

"You're very lucky to be with us at all," he assured Ismet. "That diving bell nearly finished the work the strap buckle started!"

"I remember the bell coming by me," Ismet said. "What happened to it?"

"It's still on deck. The crew chained it down."

Ismet nodded. Pain like an ice pick behind his eyeballs encouraged him to stop nodding. Again he complied. He didn't want to show his disappointment that the bell was still on board.

He brought his hand slowly up to his bandaged head and gingerly fingered the thick pad that covered the left side of his head. The bunk tilted sharply and Ismet remembered why he had been on deck in the first place. His stomach knotted and the bitter taste of bile rose in his throat. He rolled over on his side and pulled his knees up. His battered head joined forces with his tortured guts in an internal assault that took no prisoners.

Perhaps, he prayed, perhaps the ship will sink! That would be lovely.

It is hard to sustain terror. Even fear gives way to fatigue. Patno's crew had finally settled into a lethargic routine. The towing had not worsened the damage and the pumps were keeping the Pacific at bay. The *19th of January* could not move on its own, but it had electric power enough to run its sonar, and if worse came to worse, it could still fight.

That thought chilled Patno. He had the ability to engage another enemy, but since he could not maneuver, he would be an easy target.

The sonarman was slumped at his console, exhausted from the exertion of both the battle and now the search for the elusive British submarine. They were pounding away with the active sonar now, seeking any large metal object.

In his current state, Patno suspected, I doubt that he could detect his ass with own hand. He stepped over behind the man and put a hand on his back.

"Hear anyone playing 'Hail Britannia,' eh?"

The man sat upright. "No, Captain," he reported, "only our companions' engines and an occasional whale fart."

Patno chuckled. At least the man had the energy to be sarcastic.

"Keep listening," Patno urged. "As soon as you find it, we go home!" Patno felt the man stiffen as the responsibility for the whole mission fell on him.

It's unfair to pressure him like that, Patno admitted to himself, but it will keep him alert.

In truth, everyone on the *19th of January* could hear the sonar blasting away. They would not be able to hear a faint return, but a close contact would ring back through the hull.

The air was becoming hot and fetid. In a few hours, at most, they would have to approach the surface and raise the snorkel. There was battery power enough to purge the air in the sub, and with the snorkel up, they could run the generators to recharge the batteries.

His only worry was that the heavy seas could worsen the damage already done to the sub. The reports from the surface indicated that the storm was moving, but slowly. Their best hope lay in finding the sunken British submarine. Then they could be towed in for repairs. Surely they could locate it. The Russian had been actively pinging on something when they had attacked. They were already in the area. It was only a matter of time.

"Captain," Jefferies's voice cracked over the intercom, "that 209's back in business!"

Merganthal pressed the intercom switch. "What's he doing, Jefferies?"

"Active pinging, sir," the sonarman answered. "He's looking for us again, but he's headed the wrong way."

"Let me know if he comes any closer," Merganthal ordered. He looked at Bob Moore, who sat in the captain's swivel chair, his hands folded on his chest. "I hope your friends return soon, Mr. Moore," Merganthal said earnestly, "otherwise—"

"Captain," Jefferies interrupted, "there's definitely something strange about that 209." He twisted in his chair, slipping off his headphones and rubbing both ears. "He's searching, but he's not turning any revolutions."

"What do you mean?" Merganthal asked.

"The only propellor noise I hear is from the surface contacts. Those surface ships must be towing that sub around!"

"Looks like their surface ships don't have the sonar to find us so deep," Moore broke in.

Merganthal chuckled. "What a sophisticated operation!" he observed.

"Sophisticated enough," Moore said, standing and stretching. He took a deep breath, then bent over, racked by a coughing fit.

"The scrubbers aren't doing much, I'm afraid," Merganthal explained. "If someone doesn't come to get us soon, all this may be academic."

"I seriously doubt that those guys pinging around out there care much if we're alive or not," Moore said, hooking his thumb aft again. "All they want is that forest full of goodies."

An odd serious look came over Merganthal. "We may have to prepare a surprise for our greedy little wog friends," he said.

Carla turned as she felt a tap on her back.

"Any contact yet?" O'Connor asked.

"Not yet," she answered. "That doesn't mean they can't hear us. We may just not be able to hear them yet."

"I hope you're right," he said, looking at the injured men crowded into the small sub. Many were unconscious, the others slipping in and out. O'Connor cradled one man's injured head on his shoulder, the blood-soaked bandage leaking onto his own coveralls.

"We'll be there soon," she assured him. "It's not a big place, but bigger than this and there'll be help on the way as soon as we dock."

"I know that this is a trite question," he said, "but—"

"What's a nice girl like me doing in a sub like this?" she finished for him. He grinned and looked away for a second.

"It's a very long story." She smiled. "When we have some time, you can buy me a drink and I'll tell you all about it."

"It's a date," he said, returning her smile.

"Land ho!" Tom Jackson called from the front bubble. Carla and King crowded up behind him. Through the gloomy water, the blinking strobe atop the mining module flashed its blue-white greeting.

"Thank God," Carla whispered. She turned back to the others. "Mr. O'Connor, we're almost home."

"Thank God, indeed," he agreed.

"How's your friend?" she asked, touching the wounded man O'Connor held. The man's cheek felt like ice. Carla pulled up first one eyelid, then the other as O'Connor shifted around to look at the man.

Carla's eyes met his. "I'm afraid we're too late for him."

O'Connor's face fell. He reached up and held the dead man's face against his own shoulder.

"Sorry, Tommy," he whispered. Carla put her hand over O'Connor's and held it there, sharing his grief and frustration.

They were still holding the dead man's head when Jackson called from the pilot's seat.

"Prepare to dock," he said, "welcome to Rock Sucker!" As the little sub settled onto the module's airlock, a weak, ragged cheer went up from the wounded men. Two minutes later they opened the airlock hatch and stepped into the mining module.

As Carla helped the wounded men from the sub, Jackson got on the station's communications.

"This is Rock Sucker!" he shouted. "Come in, DeepCore!" There was no answer. After another try, Jackson gave up and began helping the wounded men out of the sub. Carla and King made the wounded as comfortable as possible in the cramped module.

When all the wounded had been unloaded, Jackson and King began pulling the spent fuel cells from the little sub and replacing them with full ones.

"Carla, keep trying to raise DeepCore," Jackson said as he loaded the last remaining fuel cell, "I'm going back for the rest."

Carla walked over to Jackson and put her arms around his neck.

"You be careful!" she said. Jackson laughed.

"Don't worry about me," he answered, cocking his head toward the wounded men scattered all over the module, "take care of these guys."

She kissed him firmly on the lips and stepped back. "Okay"—she nodded—"scoot!" Jackson winked and stepped through the hatch, sealing it from the other side. A moment later she heard the soft whoosh as the little sub broke contact from the module.

"Why have we not found the Englishman yet?"

"Minister," Chostsa tactfully pointed out, "it is a big ocean, even when one knows where to look. We only know the general area and the rough seas make it hard to maintain a position. We are trying, but the submarine crew needs to come to the surface and they cannot surface safely here."

"Can we mark this spot so we can resume our search later?" Fido asked.

"We can, Minister," Chostsa assured him, "we will drop a sonar beacon here. We will be able to locate it easily when we return."

"How far will we need to tow the submarine for it to surface?"

"Fifty kilometers should be enough, Minister."

Fido was silent for a moment. He turned toward Chostsa with a look that made his knees weak. "Very well, Captain, order the marker dropped." Chostsa nodded and turned to go.

"Captain," Fido snapped, bringing Chostsa up short, "if this delay proves too costly, you will answer for it."

"Yes, Minister," Chostsa agreed. He slipped down the stairs to radio the freighter to drop the sonar marker.

Why don't I just shoot myself now? Chostsa asked himself, Why wait for some stranger to do it?

There was some cheering when Patno announced that they were stopping the search to surface outside the storm, but the cheers changed to groans when he added that they would resume the search as soon as possible.

"At least we will get some air!" Askart pointed out. That cheered the crew somewhat. The air inside the *19th of January* was bad now, stale and filled with the smell of sweat and fear.

"We'll surface in the lea of the freighter," Patno explained, "that should keep the wave action down enough."

"If it doesn't slam the freighter into us," Askart answered grumpily. "It is useless for us to continue this search. We do not even know if the Russian had found anything, much less where. We should go home."

"Shall I put you through to Minister Fido," Patno asked, "so you can explain your theory?"

Askart did not answer. The question was rhetorical.

"Take heart, my friend"—Patno smiled, patting his executive officer's shoulder—"we will come through this, you'll see!"

Askart managed a weak, totally unconvincing smile.

14

A soft breeze was blowing in through the louvered window as he came to her bed. Even in the dim moonlight, Carla could see his rippling muscles, the tan skin stretched over his tight flesh. As he reached for her, she could feel his excitement like an electric current on his skin.

He bent down and poked her shoulder with something hard and cold as he whispered, "Greetings!"

Carla woke to the sight of a particularly ugly submachine gun staring her in the face. Behind it, a black-clad man stood smiling at her.

"Yaahh," she screamed, falling backward out of the chair onto the metal deck. The stranger towered above her, the gun propped now on his hip.

"Who, who, what?" she stammered, her eyes darting around the room.

They had all fallen asleep. She and King had bandaged the wounded as well as they could, and fed those who could eat. Fear, fatigue, and tension finally caught up with them and both she and King had fallen asleep after trying again to reach their friends at DeepCore.

"I'm Gunnery Sergeant Miller," the dark figure said, reaching down to help her up. "We're Navy SEALs, we're here to help you."

Around the room, half a dozen other men in dark coveralls were checking the wounded, speaking softly into thin microphones that hovered next to their mouths.

"How the hell did you get in here?" Carla asked incredulously.

"We parked our DSRV on top of the lock and walked in," he replied. "You guys were dead to the world."

"I'm afraid some of us are dead, period," a voice from the next room answered. O'Connor stepped out and snapped a quick salute.

"Corbin O'Connor, Royal Navy," he introduced himself. The man in black returned the salute.

"These are my men," O'Connor went on, "from Her Majesty's submarine *Revenge*. We hit a drifting mine and sunk a ways from here. These good people came to our rescue."

"We picked up fragments of messages," Miller explained. "We couldn't exactly figure out what was up, so we came looking for you."

"Looks like you came loaded for bear," Ty King said, stepping out of the control module where he had been sleeping.

"We didn't know what to expect," Miller offered. He looked around at the clusters of wounded. "Are these all the survivors?"

"Oh, hell no," Carla answered, suddenly remembering the others still trapped on the *Revenge*. She leaped to her feet. "You've got to save them!"

"We will," Miller answered, "if you can tell us where to look for 'em."

"Better than that," King said, "we'll go with you!"

"How did you get here, Sergeant?" O'Connor asked. "I mean, what did you come here in? Surely your DSRV didn't bring you all this way?"

Miller smiled. "We have our own nuclear limo," he answered. "It's called the USS *Sam Houston*."

• • •

Jackson's head dropped forward and he reflexively jerked it back up, the sudden snap pulling at the muscle in his neck.

"Fuck me!" he cursed, rubbing the back of his neck with his hand. "You have to stay awake, buddy boy," he reminded himself, "you're the only one here." He twisted his head to one side and scowled.

"You talkin' to me?" he snarled in an imitation of De Niro's twisted cabbie. "I'm the only one here!

"Ughh, Jackson," he moaned, "you're a sick puppy! You're talking to yourself and getting some answers!" He stretched up and rolled his shoulders forward, trying to work out the stiffness as he checked the compass heading. He was still on course, even after falling asleep.

Still, he knew, it wouldn't take much to get off course and never find the *Revenge* again. That unappealing idea woke him up. He checked his watch. If his speed was right, he should come up on the wrecked sub in a few minutes. Until then, he just had to hang on and keep awake.

Ahead in the gloom, a shape darker than the surrounding darkness loomed.

"Holy shit!" Jackson observed. "I almost ran right by it!" He switched on the forward lights. The lights pierced into the dark water, illuminating the dark bulbous submarine bow.

"Okay," Jackson said, "never fear, Jackson's here!" He slowed as he made his way aft along the big sub's deck. The sail loomed up into the lights.

"Heeere's Johnny!" Jackson said as he skirted the sail, looking for the emergency hatch. He was halfway down the sail when he saw the big red star painted there.

Jackson brought his little sub to a stop. This wasn't the *Revenge.* It was the Russian that had been killed as they had listened aboard the *Revenge.*

The Russian was resting on the rocky bottom, tilted slightly bow up. Jackson maneuvered slowly along the sail, looking for damage. It didn't take long to find it.

The Russian sub's outer hull was broken just behind the sail, a ragged hole gaping on the port side. He couldn't see any other damage, but there had been three loud booms.

The other holes are probably in the bottom somewhere, he assumed. Many western torpedoes were designed to go off under their target to break it apart with both the blast and the resulting air bubble, which could break a ship or a sub in half.

"You poor fuckers," he said quietly, then changed his mind. "Poor fuckers, nothing," he added, "you tried to do the same thing to us!" He kicked his little sub's speed back up and pulled up over the dead Soviet submarine.

"Suck on that, Ivan," he declared as he sped off to find his friend and the remaining survivors of the *Revenge.*

"No, I mean it," Jefferies insisted, "they're leaving!"

Merganthal, standing next to the sonar station, listened on the headset.

"That splash must have been a marker," Moore guessed.

"Are they all leaving?" Merganthal asked. Jefferies nodded.

"I believe so," he agreed. "If they left someone here, he'd have to use his engines to maintain his position."

"Unless he moored to that marker they threw," Moore suggested.

"In any event," Merganthal observed, "we seem to have a respite." He looked down at Jefferies. The man was exhausted.

"Jefferies, get some sleep," he ordered. "We can listen for their return. They are a pretty noisy crew. We'll come get you if anything turns up."

"Aye, sir," Jefferies answered, slumping forward onto his console. Merganthal poked him. "Find a dry rack and get some real sleep!" Jefferies nodded, stood stiffly, and staggered down the ladder toward the remaining crew quarters.

"He's a good sailor," Moore said, slipping into the still warm chair.

"They're all good," Merganthal asserted, "if they weren't, they wouldn't be here!" Merganthal's face was drawn and, to Moore's thinking, deadly white.

"You should get some sleep, too, Captain," he suggested.

"No, I'll be fine," Merganthal argued, "I—" Exhaustion settled over the captain like a fog. "Well, maybe for a few minutes." He turned to the other crew in the command center. "I'll be in my cabin."

Merganthal gave Moore a weak smile as he started for his quarters, then stopped and chuckled.

"I guess I don't have any quarters anymore," he remembered. He walked back to the ladder and disappeared below as Moore slipped on the sonar headphones.

The captain was barely out of sight when Moore suddenly stiffened.

"Captain," he shouted, "we have company!" Moore searched the panel, found the button that activated the sonar speaker, and pressed it. A loud bell-like ping rang out as Merganthal's head reappeared up the ladder.

He'd missed it on the first pass. Without any landmarks, relying only on his compass, he had drifted off to one side. When intuition had turned to real fear, he had begun a circular search, using the little active sonar and sounding the electric horn he and Ty King had mounted on the little sub.

The horn had originally just been for laughs. He and King would sound it when they were docking at DeepCore, then yell something stupid over the comm net. It hadn't taken long for the joke to wear thin with the DeepCore crew and they had not used it for weeks. Now it was an underwater signature that Bob Moore would not mistake.

The loud booming ping had assured him he was in the right neighborhood. It didn't take long after that to find the *Revenge.*

After docking, he banged on the hatch, which promptly opened. The air that rushed out was even nastier than he remembered.

"Hi, guy!" Bob Moore quipped as Jackson dropped down onto the wet deck.

"Geez," Jackson complained, ducking out of the water dripping from the hatch, "this place smells like an old gym locker!"

"Sorry, the Air-Wick gave out," Moore said, laughing. "You ready to take these guys off, or do you want to catch some Z's?"

"I'm okay," Jackson assured him, "I got some of these babies to help keep me awake." He fished in his pocket and produced a handful of tiny white pills the size of saccharin tablets. Each tablet had a cross embossed in it.

"Where the fuck did you get those?" Moore demanded. DeepCore had a rigid, draconian policy on drugs.

Jackson smiled. "Confiscated them from a mechanic on the last shakedown!" he answered. "I been saving them for an emergency!"

Moore scowled at him. "If I'd known you had them," he insisted, "you'd have had an emergency!"

Jackson simply smiled, split the handful of pills into two handfuls, and gave one to Moore.

"Just in case!" he said. Moore made no effort to stifle his annoyance, but poured the pills into his breast pocket and buttoned the flap over them as Merganthal walked up behind them.

"Are you ready, Mr. Jackson?" Merganthal asked.

"Anytime, Captain." Jackson beamed.

"Excellent!" Behind Merganthal, the crew was lining up to board the rescue sub.

"Leave your escape gear here," Jackson told the crew. "There's not enough room in the sub for it and you won't need it anyway."

Grumbling broke out in the line and a voice from the rear shouted, "They told us we'd never need the bleedin' stuff before, too, didn't they?"

"And I'm tellin' ya now," Jackson answered, "leave it!" The grumbling continued.

"Hey, trust me!" he shouted to loud catcalls and verbal abuse as the crew slipped off their rescue hoods and queued up to enter the little sub. Jackson preceded them up the ladder.

As each man entered the sub, a stout petty officer named Banner entered their name on a ledger. When the last of the crew climbed aboard, Banner followed after carefully entering his own name on the list.

"Okay," Jackson shouted from inside, "that's it for this run! How many do we have left?"

Banner stuck his head down through the hatch. The only two men left outside the rescue sub were Merganthal and Moore.

"Come on, then, Skipper," Banner urged, "there's lots of room!"

"The hell there is!" Jackson hollered. "Sorry, Bob, I'll have to make another run!"

"Get out of here!" Moore shouted up through the hatch. "We'll wait for the next car!" Loud protests issued from the rescue sub. The British sailors were not about to leave their captain behind. Merganthal cut short the protests.

"Shut up in there!" he shouted above the din. "You're on board Mr. Jackson's submarine now! He gives the orders and you follow them! Understood?"

A weak chorus of "Aye, ayes" sounded from above.

"All right, then," Merganthal ordered, "get out of here."

"I'll be back, Bob," Jackson called as Banner dropped the hatch and cut off any more conversation. Merganthal reached up and shut the *Revenge*'s hatch, dogging it down tight. A moment later the two men heard the little rescue sub break its seal on the missile boat.

Merganthal's face was instantly covered with relief. "Thank God they're on their way!" he said, sinking to the floor and leaning against the wet bulkhead.

"Jackson's good," Moore assured him, "he'll get 'em through."

Merganthal sat looking up at the hatch for a moment, then struggled to his feet. "Would you join me in a spot of brandy?" he asked.

Moore laughed. "Glad to!" The two men descended to the narrow officers' wardroom. There was a few inches of water on the deck in the room, the result of a tiny leak that now shot a needle-fine jet of salt water across the polished table. Merganthal turned his back to the spray as he crossed to a serving area recessed into the bulkhead. He reached into his shirt and pulled out a light chain on which hung two keys.

One of the keys was a flat T-shaped red metal bar that ended in a long key. Merganthal used the other key, a smaller brass model, to unlock the cabinet. He reached in and produced a bottle of VSOP and two small glass snifters. He hugged the brandy to his body as he returned through the spray, keeping the bottle safe from contamination.

"Here we are," he said, handing Moore a glass and pulling

the stopper from the bottle. He poured a generous slug of the tawny liquid into each glass and carefully replaced the stopper.

"To our rescuers from DeepCore!" Merganthal toasted, raising his glass in salute.

"To the valiant crew of the *Revenge,*" Moore answered, "and her courageous captain." They touched the glasses together and tossed back the fiery liquor.

"Whoa!" Moore exclaimed as an internal tremor shook him. "This is strong stuff!"

"Mostly use it for men who fall overboard or have to swim in the cold water for some reason," Merganthal explained, "brings 'em right around!" He finished the bit left in his glass.

"Here," he suggested, "let's take the bottle with us! Too wet down here for my taste!"

Moore followed as Merganthal led the way back up to the command center.

Once there, Merganthal slumped into the sonarman's chair and flipped some switches on the console. A high, faint humming issued from a speaker up on the bulkhead.

"Might as well listen the easy way," Merganthal suggested, "I doubt that we'll hear anything for a while."

Moore nodded and leaned over, extending his empty glass. Merganthal refilled it with the potent brew. As Moore took another, smaller sip, Merganthal looked around the now deserted command center.

"I'm going to miss her, you know," he said, unable to conceal the sadness in his voice, "she's been a good boat." Moore nodded. He had been a Navy man long enough to know the attachment any crewman can feel for his ship. He knew that captains were virtually married to their vessels.

"Here," Merganthal said, suddenly rising from the sonarman's chair, "you keep this. I have something to do before

I have any more." He handed Moore the bottle and started for the ladder, then turned.

"This will take some time," he cautioned, "but I expect there to be some of that left when I'm finished!"

Moore held the bottle up in a silent toast as Merganthal disappeared.

15

Askart stood gulping huge lungfuls of air. He choked as a blast of spray hit his open mouth.

"Be careful you do not drown, Mr. Askart," Patno suggested.

Askart laughed, spitting out the seawater. "Never has air tasted so sweet before!" he said, drawing another deep breath.

"How right you are," Patno agreed. The air was indeed a fresh contrast to the dank miasmal atmosphere below.

The *19th of January* was wallowing in the tall swells, pulling at first one, then the other of its two towlines. The patrol boats were going slow, keeping the strain on the sub as small as possible.

On deck, several of the crew were busy welding over the damaged deck plates. Most of the damage could not be reached so easily. It could only be repaired in port, if then.

The submarine's purchase had not included many spare parts. Luckily, the *19th of January* was a good boat and required few repairs. Patno did not even know if there was a replacement propellor available closer than Jakarta. His greatest fear was that the submarine was not repairable, leaving him without a ship or a job.

A cry from the repair crew drew his attention. One of the repair party had slipped on the wet deck and burned another man with the welding torch. The burned man had fallen overboard.

Tied to the deck by a lifeline, the man was floundering in the water, trying to keep his head up as the submarine pulled him along. The other members of the repair party were hauling on the line, trying to bring him back on deck. The repairs would have to wait until the man was retrieved.

"Mr. Askart," Patno snapped, "radio the minister's patrol boat and ask them to pick up our wounded man." Askart dropped down the ladder, leaving Patno alone on the bridge.

Looking aft, Patno watched the retreating storm. It covered the entire horizon to the north. On its edges, lightning flashed, lighting up the dense swirling cloud mass.

Here, running south away from the storm, the water was calmer, but the waves were still high, still agitated and heaving from the storm's pull.

Spray broke over the sail again, soaking his head and neck. Patno felt the cold water trickle down the back of his jacket. It felt good, somehow.

Perhaps it merely feels good to be topside in the real world, he mused. Submerged, they were in a dry, sterile world of echoes and flickering cathode images where life was a boring, mind-numbing routine until death came whining in on high-pitched screws. Up here, the sea was wet and cold, the sky and the rain real on the horizon.

Askart's head appeared in the hatch. "Captain, the patrol boat refuses to come pick up the wounded man."

"Very well," Patno snorted as Askart scrambled up the ladder to the bridge, "get him back on board, take him below, and treat his injury as well as possible."

"Yes, sir," Askart replied as he climbed up over the bridge and began to climb down the side of the sail.

Ahead, a large wave broke over the bow. Patno leaned over the edge of the bridge and grabbed Askart's right hand.

"Hold on, Mr. Askart!" Patno shouted as the wave surged over the deck. Askart vanished, hidden by the foaming wall of water that swept past. Patno braced his feet inside the bridge and grabbed his exec's wrist with both hands. Askart had a death grip on the welded steel rung, but Patno could feel the man's body move as the water tore at him. In two seconds that seemed like hours, the wave was past and Askart emerged, soaking wet and clinging to two of the rungs. He flailed with his feet for a second until he found his footing, then looked up at the captain.

"Thank you, sir!" he gasped, shaking the water from his face. Another cry from aft made them look back at the repair party.

The wave had knocked everyone there off their feet. The welding equipment was hanging over the side of the boat, dangling from the gas hoses. The men on deck were all looking aft, too.

There, a broken lifeline streamed behind the boat.

"Mr. Askart," Patno said, looking back down at the drenched officer, "belay that last order and come back up to the bridge."

Another man dead, Patno fumed as Askart climbed back up into the bridge and stood shivering and dripping beside him, and for what?

"Go below," Patno snapped, "get dry again and report back up here!" Askart disappeared down the ladder into the submarine.

"How many, O Feared Minister?" Patno muttered at the dark ocean. "How many will you kill in this insane search? All of us?"

He closed his eyes and took a deep breath of the cold air. "I hope we fail, Exalted One," Patno murmured. "If we succeed, you and Mad Mowati may kill the whole nation."

A loud pop behind him caught his attention. The repair crew was back at work on the hull welding, literally, for their lives.

• • •

"Jesus Christ!" Jackson screamed as the loud *ba-waong!* echoed through the little sub.

Ba-waong! Another loud sonar ping shook through them. Jackson jerked back the sub's throttle, letting it coast to a stop in the water.

"Keep it quiet back there," he hissed over his shoulder, "we need to try to hide if we can!" Jackson peered through the dark water, vainly trying to see the source of the powerful sonar. Behind him, Jefferies slid up against the back of the pilot's chair.

"I think that's one of yours!" he whispered. Jackson looked around at the sonarman.

"How can you tell?" he hissed. "Do they sound that much different?" Jefferies's eyes suddenly got wide as his mouth dropped open.

"*Aaayyhh!*" he cried, pointing over Jackson's shoulder. Jackson turned back in time to see the huge dark nose of the submarine emerge from the gloom dead ahead.

Jackson slammed the throttle forward, pulling back so hard on the joystick control that he was afraid it would break off in his hand. The little sub shot upward as the enormous bulk slid below them. Jackson jerked the joystick to the right, turning away from the long hull to avoid the sail that was still hidden in the gloom. Seconds later, the sail swept by, spinning Jackson's small sub in its turbulence.

"Fuck me running!" Jackson exclaimed, fighting to regain control of the twisting craft.

His struggle was interrupted by a voice that came over the VHF radio.

"Rock Sucker," the voice said calmly, "this is USS *Sam Houston.* Do you read? Over."

Jackson grabbed the radio mike with his left hand, still working the joystick to regain control of his little vessel.

"This is Rock Sucker," he answered testily. "You nearly fuckin' rammed us, *Sam Houston*. Over."

The conversation was drowned out by loud cheering that broke out as the British crew realized that they were safe at last.

"Keep it down!" Jackson yelled over the din. "Say again, *Sam Houston*!"

"Are you equipped to dock with our airlock?" the voice asked.

"Roger that!" Jackson replied. "We can dock with anything!"

After a brief pause, the voice came back. "Please maneuver aft of our sail and set down over the red hatch."

"Roger, *Sam Houston*," Jackson answered, "with pleasure!"

As he approached the missile room door, Moore heard muffled cursing. Peering inside, he saw Merganthal perched up on a catwalk that ran between the two rows of missile launch tubes. Merganthal was sucking on a knuckle. Below him, a skein of thin wires dangled from an open panel on the tall orange launch tube.

"Never was too mechanical!" he called down to Moore, wiped the knuckle on his coveralls, and thrust his head back inside the open panel.

"What exactly are you up to?" Moore asked, walking carefully to avoid tangling his feet in the welter of wires.

"If you are right about our friend up there wanting these warheads for himself," Merganthal answered, pulling his head back out of the tube, "I thought I'd arrange a surprise for his minions, just in case they manage to get in here."

The pattern of the wiring strewn around suddenly became clearer. A bundle of wires led to a panel on the missile tube itself.

"Let me guess," Moore said, "if anyone tries to get into the missile room, the whole place goes up."

"Correct!" Merganthal beamed. He held up one of the wires trailing from the panel. "I'm wiring the launch tube hatches. If any of them are opened, they'll get a rather nasty surprise."

"How nasty?" Moore asked.

"Sixty kilotons worth," Merganthal answered proudly. He patted the tube. "If we still had the old A-3s, they'd get a two-hundred-kiloton surprise!"

"Somehow, I think sixty will be plenty," Moore speculated. "By the way, do you know that we're sitting right on top of a big fault line here?"

"Are we, now?" Merganthal answered.

"Uh-huh," Moore went on, "this trench we're in is actually the fault line itself. It sunk after the last big movement."

"When was that?" Merganthal asked, twisting two wires together.

"About a hundred years ago," Moore answered as Merganthal pinched the two twisted wires with a pair of needle-nosed pliers and disappeared back into the tube.

"When it went last time," Moore continued, raising his voice so Merganthal could hear, "about half of the islands that make up Manawatu disappeared."

Merganthal pulled back out of the tube. "Pity that the rest didn't go as well."

"Don't be mean, now," Moore replied, "I've heard people say that about England, too."

"Who?"

"My Irish uncles," Moore answered.

"They would." Merganthal shined his flashlight around inside the launch tube, inspecting his wiring job. "There," he observed, hoisting himself up on the catwalk. He took three steps to the metal ladder and climbed back down to the deck.

"Did you bring the brandy with you?" he asked as he reached the last rung and turned to Moore.

"No," Moore replied, "I left it in the command center."

"Pity"—Merganthal smiled—"the next step is the hard part." He pointed to a long panel that ran along the first two launch tubes. "That's the launch tube status panel," he explained. "I have to wire into each hatch cover, so that if one is opened, the trap is sprung." He wiped his hands on his coveralls. "This will be the tricky part."

"I think I'll leave you to it, then," Moore said, looking down the rows at the sixteen long launch tubes, "this stuff makes me nervous enough as it is. I don't think I want to watch you tinker with it. I'll go watch the brandy."

"Make sure there's some left for me," Merganthal insisted, "I'll need a strong belt when I finish here!"

"No shit!" Moore agreed. He retreated through the missile room door as Merganthal produced a screwdriver from his coveralls and attacked the long metal panel.

Back in the command center, Moore slumped in the chair next to the chart table. The boat was silent now, so silent that Moore could hear the faint ringing that was always in his ears. The ringing was the result of too many hours spent on the weapons range and standing behind transport planes as they warmed up their engines.

The military issued earplugs and encouraged their use, but the plugs rarely found their way into a G.I. ear canal. Moore smiled, remembering the last reunion of the Special Operations Group Association. The most common response to any question was "What?" or "Huh?" Partial deafness was the hallmark of all combat veterans.

Here, in this silent metal tube, the ringing in his ears was like the dial tone on a cheap Third World telephone.

Fatigue settled over him. Moore put his arms on the chart table and laid his head on them. In less than a minute, he was sound asleep.

He woke to the sound of glass clinking on glass. Looking up, he spotted Merganthal, now attired in a dark blue parka, pouring two fingers of brandy into his glass.

"So," Merganthal quipped, "wakened from our nap, are we?"

"Yeah" Moore answered groggily, "I had this terrible dream! I dreamed that I was trapped in this old English submarine and forced to live on scones and warm beer." He looked from side to side. "Oh, God! It wasn't a dream!"

"Worse than that," Merganthal shot back, "the movie tonight is a double feature—*Gray Lady Down* and *The Hunt for Red October*!"

"Agghh!" Moore wailed, letting his head thump back down on the chart table.

"Care for another toddy?" Merganthal asked.

"I'd care for one of those nice coats," Moore replied, rubbing both arms with his hands. "It's colder than a petty officer's heart in here!" For the first time, he noticed his own breath fogging as he spoke.

"Right behind you," Merganthal pointed.

Sure enough, there was another parka on the deck behind his chair. Moore slipped it on and jammed his hands into the pockets.

"How long was I out?" he asked as Merganthal poured some brandy into Moore's glass.

"Don't know, really," the captain answered, shaking his head. "To be honest with you, I'm rather losing track of time since the lads left. I think it took me two or three hours to wire up the missile room, but I didn't really check."

"You got it all booby-trapped?"

Merganthal smiled. "Any attempt to get at those missiles will cause this wonderful ship to self-destruct in the most spectacular fashion."

Moore raised his glass in a toast. "Let us be far from here if and when that event occurs!"

"Amen," Merganthal agreed.

16

"Captain," Askart said as he climbed back up onto the pitching bridge, "we have been ordered to submerge again."

Patno did not answer, but stood looking at the storm, now dead ahead of them. They had turned back north an hour before.

"The minister wants to begin the search again as soon as possible," Askart continued. "We were able to repair some of the damage to our hull, but we are still leaking in the engineering spaces. So far the pumps are keeping up with it."

"And the batteries?" Patno asked.

"They are still damaged as before," Askart replied, "but we have enough electric power to operate most of the systems."

Patno stood looking at the horizon for a moment. "What do you see, Mr. Askart?" he asked.

Askart looked quickly to the side. "I see the two patrol craft that are towing us," he said, ticking off his observations, "and the typhoon ahead of us."

"Mark it all well," Patno advised. He gave Askart a cheerless smile. "With luck, we will see it again soon!" The captain dropped down the ladder, leaving Askart on the bridge.

He looked around again, this time studying the waves, the steel-gray sky, and the storm ahead. Askart suddenly felt very small. His submarine and the two patrol boats were mere specks on the huge sea. Even the freighter seemed a toy in the huge waves.

A chill ran through him as he looked at the storm ahead. Askart shook it off and dropped down into the hatch, pulling the heavy hatch cover down behind him. Once in the command center, he felt better. In here, he seemed large and powerful.

The deck tilted slightly as the *19th of January* slipped beneath the waves again. The wallowing stopped as the sub leveled off under the towering waves.

In the command center, Patno was on the radio.

"Yes, Minister," the captain said, "we are ready to continue the underwater search. Yes, Minister, I understand." He handed the headset back to the operator and faced Askart.

"We will, once more, search for the sunken submarine until we find it or until it becomes unbearable in here again."

Askart nodded. He had expected nothing less. He looked over at the sonar operator, who already had his Krupp Atlas CSU 3-4 sonar system warmed up.

"Commence active sonar sweep," Askart ordered the man. The first ping sounded less than a second later. As he stood watching the sonar operator, Askart wondered how many hours they would spend this way, probing the depths for a sunken vessel whose whereabouts were increasingly obscure. His dark ruminations were interrupted by the sonarman's shout.

"Contact!" he shouted. "Deep! Starboard side!"

"Already?" the captain asked, stepping over by the sonar console. "Can you classify?"

The sonar operator studied his scope for a moment, then looked up at the captain. "No, sir, I cannot classify it," he admitted, "but it is big!"

The captain turned to Askart. "Relay this contact to the minister." He looked back down at the flickering image on the screen. "Perhaps God has smiled on us for once."

"Inshallah!" the operator agreed.

When the round red hatch opened, Jackson looked down into the big sub and stared openmouthed at Carla's smiling face.

"Hi, sailor," she said brightly, "new in town?"

"What in the name of God are you doing here?" he asked.

"Come on down here and I'll tell you all about it!" she urged. Jackson stepped down through the hatch onto the ladder and jumped down in front of his friend. Behind Carla stood two smiling men in navy khaki and another somber man in a black jumpsuit.

"Tom Jackson, UnderSea Corporation," Jackson introduced himself.

The older of the two men in khaki stepped around Carla.

"Ward Beecher," the man introduced himself, "captain of the *Sam Houston*." He pointed back toward the others. "This is Milt Tanner, my exec, and Sergeant Miller of the SEALs."

"Permission to come aboard, sir," Jackson said, trying to remember his naval courtesy.

Beecher laughed. "You and your passengers are welcome, Mr. Jackson. Have them come aboard, we have some hot coffee and food for them."

This conversation, overheard by those still in the rescue sub, was met by a cheer of approval. One by one, the British sailors climbed down the ladder and were led aft by Lt. Tanner.

"Where's Bob?" Carla asked as the last of the crew descended. "And the British captain?"

Jackson looked down at the deck. "There wasn't room," he answered, "they stayed on the *Revenge*."

Beecher, standing behind Carla, interrupted, "You mean you've still got people on that sub?"

"That's right," Jackson answered, "but if you'll take this bunch, I'll go back and get them!"

Beecher grinned. "I've got a better idea, Mr. Jackson," he suggested, "we'll drop your passengers off at the mining station and then take you back there!" He held up his palms and looked around. "After all, we can get there and back a bit quicker."

"What about my little sub?" Jackson asked.

"The SEALs can secure it to the deck," Beecher assured him. Behind the captain, Miller, the dour man in the black coveralls, nodded.

"No problem," he said flatly, "we'll get right on it." He disappeared forward down the passageway.

"Come on, Tom," Carla urged, taking his arm and leading him aft, "you need some food, too."

He let himself be led away.

In the spacious troop compartment, the British crew was unhappy.

"See here," one of them was complaining, "we should go back right now and get Captain Merganthal and the Yank!" The others were grumbling their agreement as they gulped the hot cups of coffee. Tanner was listening to them patiently, shaking his head.

"I'm sorry," he apologized, "but we have orders to bring you guys back first. As soon as we drop you off, we'll go after the other two."

Before they could object further, Tanner explained. "It's not our idea," he assured the angry sailors, "we got orders. As soon as you're safe, we can go back. Not until."

The British crew was obviously not satisfied, but they understood orders. As Jackson entered the room, they all stood and gathered around him, clapping him on the back, shaking his hand, and staring at his beautiful companion.

"We'll get your captain back," Jackson promised them, "and our boss, too." He looked over at Tanner. "Right?"

"Dead right," Tanner answered.

17

"Careful, you fools," Palatin screamed, "do you want to destroy it before it even gets in the water?" He spun toward Whitcox. "Are these apes incapable of understanding even simple instructions?" he shrieked. "The minister will not be pleased if they wreck the bell before I can even have a look below!"

Whitcox, his jacket collar turned up against the cold wind, called to the deck foreman and motioned him over. The foreman, a hulking, hairy brute of a man, lumbered over. Palatin watched the two men as the captain again explained the delicacy of the diving equipment.

The captain was a nondescript man. Palatin would not have even noticed him on the street. The foreman was a gorilla. He stood with his bulging arms folded on his chest, wearing only a thin T-shirt and canvas pants against the increasingly chilly breeze.

The deck gang was hoisting the diving bell over the side with one of the cargo booms. Palatin was supervising a dry run to make sure the deck crew knew what needed to be done. They would drop the bell down to five hundred feet, leave it for ten minutes, then bring it back up on deck. Palatin would then check it for leaks and damage.

This would be their only practice, the only time to check the equipment for damage or malfunction. The bell had not been used for years. Although it had been stored in a warehouse and protected from the elements, the effects of age were hard to predict.

Once inside the bell, he would not be able to fix any damage or to correct the crew's mistakes. If the bell malfunctioned or the crew made any serious errors, he would not survive.

Fear of his own death terrified him enough, but Palatin knew that if he failed Mowati, his whole family would suffer. The dictator was known for the depth of his animosity. If the bell failed, he knew, the intense water pressure would kill him instantly. His wife and child would suffer a slower, more agonizing fate in the bowels of Mogador prison.

That thought spurred his caution. He tried to focus on the job at hand. If this dry run was successful, he would go down to investigate the sonar return.

"Captain," he said as the big dock foreman went back to his gang, "are you sure you can maintain a constant position in this sea?"

Whitcox looked past him at the rolling seas, his eyes narrowing to slits. The wind whipped his jacket collar in his face.

"Today, perhaps," the captain replied, "tomorrow or the next day, certainly."

"Then we should tell the minister to wait until tomorrow or the next day!" Palatin urged.

Whitcox smiled and chuckled. "You do not know the minister!" he replied. "Our opinions are of no value to him." The captain locked eyes with Palatin. "We are here to do his bidding and failure is simply not permitted."

Palatin nodded. It was a grim situation, but only success would free them from it.

Malachi Fido watched from the freighter's bridge as the crew hoisted the bell over the side and lowered it into the water. The huge spool of air hose turned as the bell dropped deeper below the ship. Although he was impatient to begin the recovery phase of the operation, he understood the need to check the old equipment.

Since there was only one man skilled in the bell's operation, he could not afford to lose him at this early stage.

This early sonar contact was a blessing. After their first unsuccessful attempt, he had envisioned a long, boring search marked by increasingly frequent stoppages to allow the submarine crew to surface. He had been worried that the longer the search went on, the less efficient it would be.

There was, of course, the chance that this contact was not the British submarine at all. The Pacific was littered with wrecks, many from World War II. It would not take long to determine if this was the case. At worst, it would be a valuable practice for the time when they found the Englishman.

He had no doubt that they would find it. His only concern was removing the warheads. Mere enthusiasm would hardly be enough to get the warheads out of the submarine intact. There was only one man in Manawatu's armed forces who knew enough about nuclear submarines to be of any use, and he was down in the *19th of January*. He would have to take Patno along to inspect the submarine and determine how to get at the atomic warheads.

If this contact proved to be the Englishman, he would take Patno off the *19th of January* and keep him here on the freighter. Fido had come aboard after they had broken off the search in order to recharge their submarine's batteries.

On the deck below, the huge spool stopped. A crowd gathered along the rail, looking down at the dark water. For a moment he wondered if the bell was all right. Then the crowd pulled back from the rail and the hose spool began to turn the other way, rewinding the thick black air hose as it brought the bell to the surface.

Palatin held his breath as the bell emerged from the water and swung over above the deck. The crane operator gently set it down on the deck and the deck crew quickly chained it down onto its pallet.

As he walked up to the bell, Palatin could see that it was, at least, intact. He stepped up on the pallet and looked inside through the large observation port. There was no water inside, not even any condensation on the port. His heart leaped with relief, then crashed as the realization set in. The bell worked. Now he would have to go down in it.

"Is it operational?" Whitcox asked from behind him.

"It seems to be perfectly fine," Palatin said, turning to face the captain. "We can proceed anytime the minister wishes."

"Then prepare to go down in it," Whitcox answered, "he just told me to get on with it if the bell was operational."

Palatin took a long look around, breathing deeply to steady his nerves.

"I am ready," he confessed. Whitcox motioned two of the deck crew over to assist Palatin in getting the bell's hatch open.

The hatch was underneath the bell and surrounded by a wide circular skirt that allowed it to dock with a variety of underwater vessels and habitats. The two deckhands held the hatch up as Palatin slithered up into the bell.

Once inside, he lowered the hatch and dogged it shut. The air inside had a rubbery smell that he had forgotten since his days with the *Geographic* crew. Those days seemed like a pleasant dream now. He sat down on the folding seat and buckled the thin seat belt that would keep him in place while they swung the bell over and lowered it into the water. This done, he took the intercom headset off its hook on the wall and put it on.

"Communications check," he said, "how do you read?"

Malachi Fido's voice hissed in his ears, scaring Palatin. "We can hear you just fine," the minister said, "are you ready to proceed?"

"Yes, Minister," Palatin answered. He gave a thumbs-up signal to the crewman who was peering in through the observation port. The man disappeared and a moment later the bell lurched as the crane lifted it off its pallet and swung it over the side.

As it swung over the side, the bell turned and the freighter vanished from sight. A knot of fear formed in his stomach as the sea rose slowly up. The bell tilted sharply as it hit the water and it was suddenly dark inside the bell.

Palatin switched on the dim red instrument lights and watched as the thick surface foam gave way to dark green ocean as the bell dropped below the ship.

He quickly checked the three smaller observation ports for leaks. There was no trace of moisture on any of them and the large front port was dry as well. He scanned the small cluster of instruments. They seemed to be working. The needle in the depth gauge was creeping around the dial. The pressure in the bell was constant. Palatin winced as he remembered the one piece of equipment he had not been able to check. The emergency shut-off valve between the bell and the air hose could not be checked without disconnecting the hose. There had been no opportunity to check it onshore and he had been too sick to deal with it on board. If something cut the air hose, he would know in a second if the valve was operating. If it failed, he would have only seconds to live.

He forced that morbid thought from his mind and concentrated on the descent. The depth gauge read ninety meters when Fido spoke to him again.

"Are you there, Palatin?" Fido asked.

"Yes, Minister," Palatin answered, "everything is normal here. I am approaching one hundred meters."

"Report every fifty meters," Fido reminded him.

"Yes, Minister," he replied. He had forgotten to check in. Unbuckling his seat belt, Palatin leaned forward in the seat and peered through the thick observation port in the hatch. The water was pitch-black. Palatin switched on the four halogen lights and pointed them all down. The bright light penetrated deeply into the gloom.

He alternated his attention between the viewport and the depth gauge, calling back to the surface his depth as he descended toward the unknown contact.

The gauge read 275 meters when he felt a change in the bell's descent. Whitcox's voice came on the line.

"We are slowing your descent since you are within two hundred feet of the bottom," he explained. "We will lower you at the rate of one meter every other second now."

Palatin acknowledged the captain's message, never taking his eyes from the bottom port. His heart was racing. Whatever was down here, he would see it in a moment.

Movement caught his eye. "Slow!" he shouted into the microphone, catching himself as the bell jerked to a stop. He dropped down onto the hatch and stared out into the darkness.

"Down another meter," he ordered. This time, the movement was unmistakable. He had not been able to make it out when he stopped because the object was the same uniform black as the water around it. Now, lit by the halogen lights, it began to take shape.

"Object sighted," he reported. Fido's voice interrupted.

"What is it?" he demanded. "Can you tell?"

"It is not a surface ship," Palatin answered, "I'm sure of that. There are no barnacles or signs of rusted metal." He tried to gauge the distance to the object and could not.

"Lower another meter," he said. He could hear his own heartbeat in his ears now. The bell dropped slowly again. This time, the object stood out clearly in the lights. For a second he thought it was moving, but realized that the bell was moving through the water over the stationary object. He looked out the larger front observation port, turning two of the lights up.

Ahead in the gloom, a tall structure loomed off to the left.

"Take it up!" Palatin shouted. "Emergency!" He braced himself as the bell jerked up. The structure disappeared below.

"Stop!" he yelled. The bell rocked as it suddenly stopped. Palatin swiveled the lights back down, searching for the structure. As it slid by beneath him, he could clearly make out its oval shape, the bridge, and periscope wells on the sub's sail.

"Minister," Palatin shouted, "it is a submarine! We have found it!" He was again pushed to the bottom of the bell as it was suddenly hauled back toward the surface.

18

A tickling in his nose woke Moore from the bizarre dream. The images of brightly colored tents and medieval jesters and balladeers faded. He woke to find the fur collar of his borrowed parka under his nose, the wolverine fur tickling him. The oily, metallic smell assaulted his nose as well, bringing him fully awake.

It seemed that the emergency lights in the command center were dimmer somehow. Merganthal had turned off all the other lights in the sub to divert the battery power to the air scrubbers. It seemed that neither of those systems was doing very much now.

Merganthal was asleep, slumped over the sonar console, still wearing the headphones. Moore stretched, working the kinks out of his back. As he stood up, he yawned. The acrid taste of the sub's atmosphere caught in his throat, doubling him over as he coughed.

The noise awakened Merganthal. He sat up and pulled off the headphones, rubbing his eyes with his knuckles.

"How long were we out?" he asked. Moore looked at his ancient Rolex.

"About three hours, I guess."

Merganthal stood, yawning and scratching through the parka. "I don't know about you," he said, "but I'm suddenly quite hungry. Care for some cold breakfast?"

"I could eat," Moore answered, following Merganthal as

he slowly slumped down the ladder toward the crew's mess, using a flashlight to find his way.

In the mess hall, Merganthal found some crackers and a tin of canned meat. The two men quickly devoured the simple meal, washing it down with cold tea from an insulated steel carafe.

"I wonder when your friend will be back?" Merganthal asked, wiping the last bit of the canned meat out of the tin with a finger.

"He'll push it to the limit," Moore answered, "Tom's a compulsive kind of guy." He tipped up the last swig of tea from his china cup. "I just hope he doesn't push himself till he drops. He won't be much good to any of us if he craters. Of course, either of the two others could stand in for him. Ty King and Carla Fuentes are both good people, too."

"That Carla is quite a looker, eh." Merganthal smiled.

"Indeed she is." Moore grinned. "A lot of people underestimate her for that reason. She is one tough cookie, believe me!"

"I've heard of this DeepCore place you work for," Merganthal said, "what is it exactly?"

"It's a deep-water habitat," Moore explained, "but it's a lot more than just that. It's like an underwater industrial complex and marine research station."

"Sounds interesting," Merganthal replied. "It's privately owned, then?"

"UnderSea Corporation owns it, but we do some work for the Navy there, so the U.S. Government funnels some research money there, too." He looked off past Merganthal. "We had some trouble there a while ago," Moore remembered, "so we've got quite a bit of Navy there, now."

"Really," Merganthal asked, "what sort of trouble?"

Moore realized that he had said too much. "Oh, unwanted guests, you might say," he answered vaguely.

"Sort of like our situation here, eh?"

"Kinda," Moore observed, "but not really."

Merganthal mercifully changed the subject.

"Let's see what else there is to eat in here, shall we," he suggested, ransacking through the dark cupboard.

"If you see any rib-eyes in there," Moore hinted, "put my name on one."

" 'Fraid those would be in the freezer," Merganthal answered, "no way to cook it up, now."

"No problem," Moore quipped, "I'll just suck on it frozen. Call it a Beefcicle."

Merganthal was chuckling at his little joke when the loud thump echoed through the hull.

The dark hull loomed up out of the gloom. Palatin instructed the crane operator to move the bell over the small hatch with the white cross on it. When the hatch was directly beneath them, he called for more line. The wave action on the freighter above pulled the bell from one side to the other, but the long length of the tether dampened the effect. Crowded in next to him, Ismael, a sergeant in Fido's shadowy State Security Staff, blanched as the bell swayed.

Back on the freighter, Palatin had heard stories about the man's ruthlessness, but here, hundreds of feet below the surface of the ocean, Ismael was terrified. Above them both, literally clinging to the bell's ceiling, Malachi Fido watched the descent with his usual lack of concern.

Finally, the hatch swam toward them, only a meter below. As it slid under the bell, Palatin shouted into the microphone.

"More slack!" he shouted. "Drop us!"

The hatch seemed to rise up to meet them. The white cross was almost perfectly centered under the hatch's observation port when the bell thumped to a stop. Palatin immediately began to work a hand lever on the bottom curve of the bell.

"What is that?" Fido asked.

"A pump to pull the water out of the skirt," Palatin explained, jerking the handle back and forth. "It replaces the water with air from inside the bell. The water pressure outside forces the bell tight against the hull of the submarine so we can open the two hatches. The pressure in the submarine and in here is much less than the pressure of the water outside."

Suddenly afraid that he was talking down to the minister, Palatin shut up and continued to pump.

"How will we get in if there is no one left alive in the submarine?" Fido asked.

"That will be complicated," Palatin answered, "we will have to cut our way into the hatch with the torch." He pointed to the small acetylene set strapped under one of the folding seats. "If we cut through the hatch, we will not be able to raise the bell without flooding the submarine," he went on, "unless this is a lockout hatch." He looked up to see if the minister was following him. "If it is a lockout hatch, we will be able to come and go as we please, since there will be a second hatch below this one."

"Let us hope that is the case."

The skirt between the bell and the submarine's hull was nearly empty now. Palatin stood over the hatch and pulled the lever that moved the thick lugs, retracting them from their slots in the bell's wide bottom flange.

The hatch popped up and Palatin pulled it all the way open, securing it with a nylon strap.

"Let us see if there is air or water below the hatch," he suggested.

Palatin pulled the short metal handle off the pump, stepped down onto the British submarine's wet steel hull and banged on it with the pump handle. The blows produced a hollow ringing sound.

"Air!" Palatin smiled back up at the other two. He was reaching up for a handhold to pull himself up when the hatch opened below him and he fell on top of a very startled Englishman.

"He must have pushed that little sucker to the limit!" Moore observed as he and Merganthal made their way back to the emergency hatch.

"I expect Her Majesty will pay for any damages to it," Merganthal joked. They stood below the hatch, listening to the metallic scraping on the outside.

Finally, the hatch rang under three blows. Smiling, Merganthal reached up and spun the hatch locking ring. The lugs had barely cleared their slots when the hatch popped up and a short brown man fell screaming onto Merganthal's upturned face.

Moore stepped backward, tripped and fell over sideways, grabbing at a metal conduit to break his fall. As Moore fell, a thickset man in a greenish-brown camouflage uniform dropped through the hatch, steadying himself with one hand, a short black submachine gun clutched tightly in the other.

"Do not move!" the gunman shouted in accented English. He stepped back two steps to give himself a better firing position, both hands now on the weapon.

The three tangled men on the wet deck looked up as a spectral figure slowly lowered himself into the *Revenge* and stood carefully out of the line of fire, drawing a small pistol from his short jacket as he surveyed his two captives. The submachine gunner turned to check behind them for any other inhabitants.

A thin smile crept over the man's face. "Palatin," he said, "you must be congratulated on your capture of these men!"

He bent down toward Merganthal.

"How many of your crew are left alive?" he asked quickly as Palatin scrambled to his feet and stepped back to one side.

"None," Merganthal answered from the deck, "just us two." Moore tried to get to his feet, but the thin man gestured with his gun and Moore froze.

"Very well." The man stood and nodded slightly. "Permit me to introduce myself," he said, "I am Malachi Fido, Minister of Internal Affairs to His Excellency Sendu Mowati, President of the Republic of Manawatu, in whose waters you now reside." He smiled broadly, looking around at the submarine's interior. "You and this vessel are now my prisoners."

Moore quickly judged the distance to both men. If he could take the thin man before the ugly plug with the sub-gun could react, maybe he could get them both. This plan fell apart as the thickset man whirled and held his gun tightly back against him. Moore recognized the gun as a Czech Model 25, a simple, reliable shooter well suited to this sort of close-quarters work. The man holding it was sizing them up, too. The gun barrel shifted toward Moore's midsection.

"Palatin," the thin man said quietly, "check the rest of the ship for any other living survivors." The man on the floor with Merganthal jumped to his feet, bowed slightly, and ran off down the passageway.

"Now, gentlemen," the man said to his two captives, "please, lie down on your bellies and put your hands behind your heads!"

Merganthal looked over at him and Moore nodded. There was no point to heroics now. The squat man with the submachine gun would have no trouble killing them both before they could reach either him or his spooky boss.

"His Excellency will be happy to meet you both," the uniformed wraith assured them as they rolled over onto the wet grating and clasped their hands behind their heads. "We will have much to talk about."

Moore felt the barrel of the Model 25 slip between his legs, jamming against his crotch. A hand took his right hand and turned it down into the small of his back. Cold metal ringed his wrist as the handcuffs snapped shut. "The other!" the gunner's voice barked. Moore slid his left hand down and the man quickly snapped the cuff on it. The submachine gun's barrel jerked out from between his legs, only to be replaced by the cold steel of the other man's pistol against his neck. No one spoke as the gunner cuffed Merganthal's wrists.

When they were properly trussed up, the gunner dragged them both to their feet.

"You are making a serious mistake, my friend," Merganthal insisted. "This ship is British soil! You risk war with the United Kingdom if you try to seize it!"

"On the contrary"—the thin man laughed—"this ship is wrecked! We claim salvage on it!"

Merganthal did not respond. The four of them stood in silence for a few minutes until the other man returned from his search.

"Minister," the man named Palatin gasped, breathlessly, "there is no one else on board at all!"

"Not even any bodies?" Fido asked.

"None!" Palatin replied.

"You searched the entire ship?"

"All of it, Minister," he answered, "except the rooms that were locked."

"Flooded," Merganthal explained.

"Well," Fido said, holstering his pistol, "let us go up to our ship." He smiled at the two handcuffed men. "We have much to talk about."

"We have nothing to say to you!" Merganthal insisted.

"We will see about that." Fido laughed. The five men crowded into the bell, Palatin coming last and latching the hatch according to Merganthal's instructions.

The trip to the surface was rapid.

Plena Whitcox watched the bell emerge from the water and swing back over the deck on the end of the boom. On deck, a squad of S.S.S. troops stood waiting, their rifles ready. As the bell set down on the pallet, the soldiers ringed it. Seconds later, the hatch opened and two men, their hands bound behind them, fell to the deck, struggled out from under the pallet, and stood blinking on deck.

Fido and his goon bodyguard followed. Palatin was the last man out and he immediately went to work inspecting the bell. As the troops led the two men away, Fido headed for the bridge. Several minutes later he appeared, issuing orders to Whitcox's crew.

"Captain," he ordered, "I will return to our base at once! I have prison—er—guests, that His Excellency will want to meet immediately!"

"I shall order the group to return at once, Minister," Whitcox answered. Fido held up his hand.

"No," he corrected Whitcox, "you, the *19th of January,* and two of the patrol boats will remain on station here. I do not wish to lose this location!" He looked out at Palatin, who was now washing off the bell with fresh water.

"Captain Patno will be going down in the bell to inspect the wrecked submarine," Fido went on. "Give him all the support he requires." With that, Fido turned and left the bridge.

"Yes, Minister," Whitcox answered the man's retreating back.

19

Merganthal woke slowly, the pain in his head returning with a throbbing that felt like the sandbag was hitting him again. He tried to sit up, but the pain became blinding and he fell over again on the dirty bunk.

"Take it easy, Captain," Moore said, stepping over to lift Merganthal's feet back up on the bunk, "how's the head?"

"Feels like someone's driving a spike into it," Merganthal whispered.

"I'll say one thing for these suckers," Moore said, standing up on the bunk to look out the narrow windows, "these guys don't waste any time."

Merganthal made a noise. "Too bloody right about that," he murmured.

His Excellency Sendu Mowati had not made any bones about his desire. When Fido had brought them ashore, Mowati had met them at the heliport. Without so much as a by-your-leave, he had ordered Merganthal interrogated about the missiles. Moore had played like he was one of *Revenge*'s officers, an American officer on an exchange program with the British. He claimed to be an engineer with no knowledge of the missiles.

So far, that story had kept him from the same punishment inflicted on Merganthal.

Moore leaned down next to Merganthal's head. "How long are you going to hold out on 'em?" he whispered.

Merganthal managed a weak smile. "They get the whole story the next time they ask!" Merganthal had held out against their interrogation, not wanting to seem too eager to give them the knowledge that would lead to the destruction of the submarine. He would let them think that their own error had caused the sub to blow up. There would be no one left from the salvage crew to dispute that theory.

The sound of boots in the corridor stopped their conversation. Moore looked up to see Ismael grinning at them through the bars.

"Come, Englishman," he cackled, "it is time to play again! We have a new game for you this time!" Two jailers opened the cell door and dragged Merganthal to his feet. Ismael kept his Czech machine gun trained on Moore as the jailers led the stumbling captain from the cell.

"So, American," Ismael taunted him, "you are having a good rest, eh?" Moore did not answer, but stood looking up through the window slit at the blue sky outside as the cell door slammed shut again.

"If the Englishman will not tell us what we need," Ismael predicted, "we will ask you. Perhaps you will remember more than you think!" He laughed and disappeared, following the jailers.

"Oh, Tommy," Moore moaned, plopping heavily on the rough bunk, "why couldn't you have gotten back a little sooner?"

Both he and Merganthal had lost track of the time after they fell asleep, but he had hoped that Tom Jackson would make it back in time to rescue them before these pond scum had time to find them. The pond scum had been quick.

"No point in beating yourself over this," Moore reminded himself, "there are plenty of guys here who will be happy to beat you!"

"You see, Captain," Fido explained, "the current will pass through you, increasing in power until you see the light of reason and tell us what we want to know, or until your testicles and ears are burned away!"

Merganthal felt the cold metal wire bite into his scrotum as one of Fido's torturers wound it again and again around him, forcing his testicles farther down into the fleshy sack.

He gasped as his two gonads ran out of room and the wire began to compress them. Satisfied with the installation, the torturer reached across to the transformer, took one of the two alligator clamps, and clipped it onto the wire.

This done, he took the other clamp and clipped it to Merganthal's right ear. The metal clamp bit into his ear and Merganthal could feel the warm blood running slowly into his ear canal from the small cuts.

"Perhaps a small demonstration will help you understand the process," Fido suggested. He stepped over to the transformer and turned the dial up to its lowest setting. He turned to Merganthal and raised his eyebrows as he pressed a toggle next to the dial.

Searing pain shot through his balls and crotch. His whole body began to twitch, fighting to escape the pain that traveled up through his belly and chest, up his neck to his ear. The ear felt like it was on fire. Merganthal strained at the leather straps that held him tightly on to the steel grid.

Subhuman sounds issued from his throat and it took a second for Merganthal to realize that he was making them. The whole world seemed to condense down to the pain that fried him from his crotch to his head.

Suddenly the pain stopped. Merganthal's head fell over toward Fido who stood with his finger just off the toggle switch.

"See," the bastard crooned, "now that wasn't so bad, was it?"

A wave of nausea swept over Merganthal. If that was the lowest setting, then the damn thing really would burn his ears off and his bollocks, too. It was nearly time to give them what they wanted.

Fido turned the dial up one notch and smiled at him. "Now," he began, "how do we remove the warheads from the submarine?"

Merganthal took a quick breath. "Fuck you!" he answered.

Fido's finger moved on the switch and the world turned to pain again. This time, the searing current was so strong, Merganthal could not open his eyes. He seemed to see the electricity running through him and tried to pull his mind away from it. It was not possible.

I waited too long, he cried inside as the pain ate him up, I waited too long! After an eternity in hell, the pain ceased. At least the current ceased. Merganthal's whole body hurt now, both from the electricity and from the terrible involuntary muscle spasms the current produced.

"Please," he begged, "please, no more!" He jerked his head toward Fido, tears running from his eyes. "I'll tell you everything! Please!"

"I'm glad, Captain," Fido answered, his voice dripping with compassion, "I'm very glad." He stepped to Merganthal's side and patted his face. "I am very impressed with you, Captain," he went on, "most people see the light after the demonstration. You are a courageous man. No one could fault you for your decision."

Merganthal felt the straps come off his wrists and ankles. Two of the interrogators grabbed his arms and pulled him upright. He could feel someone pulling up his pants as he passed out.

He woke in a small room, his head on a metal desk. His arms were handcuffed behind him again. Keeping his head on the metal desktop, he looked around. There was nothing in the room but the desk and two straight-backed chairs. There was a mirror on one wall that Merganthal suspected was a one-way glass. He tried to sit up, every muscle in his body protesting the effort. It even hurt to breathe. The breath caught in his chest and he was instantly racked by a coughing fit that ached deep in his lungs.

He eased his face back down onto the cool metal desk and drifted into that fugue state between consciousness and sleep.

The sound of the metal bolt turning in the door woke him.

Fido, dressed in a crisp white naval uniform, stepped into the room. He plugged a telephone that he was carrying into an outlet in the wall and sat down.

"Feeling better, Captain?" he asked casually. Merganthal did not answer, but sat up again, ignoring his body's protests.

"I want you to tell me how to remove the warheads from the missiles on your submarine," Fido asked again.

Merganthal cautiously took another deep breath, then exhaled slowly. He closed his eyes and dropped his head forward on his chest.

"First," he began, "you switch the launch panel status to Test Mode in order to open the outer missile tube door."

20

"Comrade Captain," Somolov said through the door, "we have reached our firing position."

The door opened and Vortmet motioned Somolov into his cabin.

"Somolov," the captain began, "we have never fired a nuclear missile before." He poured a cup of hot tea from a small samovar that sat in a niche in the wall and gestured to Somolov to help himself. As Somolov poured his cup, Vortmet went on.

"I want to conduct two firing drills each day and I want the political officer there with you for every drill." Somolov smiled. Menchikov, the political officer, was a constant irritant to the others, as were all political officers. They had the power to repeal orders and to communicate independently with base, circumventing the captain.

On nuclear armed ships, they had even more power, since the nuclear warheads were under their control and could not be fired without their participation.

"Such a rigorous schedule will not please Comrade Menchikov," Somolov observed. "It will interfere with his snooping around the crew's mess and peeking under their mattresses for contraband copies of *Penthouse* magazine."

Vortmet laughed, remembering the flap that Menchikov had created on their visit to Japan. An American submarine, the *Oklahoma City,* had been in port, too, and the two captains had arranged a friendship visit between ships. The enterprising sailors from Vortmet's submarine had traded hats, belt buckles, and shoulder patches for American cigarettes, cassette tapes, and pornographic magazines.

Menchikov had found one of the magazines, *Penthouse,* and thrown a fit, insisting that the sailor under whose mattress he had found the prohibited literature be court-martialed.

Vortmet had carefully examined the evidence. One of the articles in the *Penthouse* was extremely critical of the U.S. military and American foreign policy. That article clearly made the magazine politically correct. Vortmet had refused to arrest the sailor. Menchikov had been furious.

Menchikov's only duty in missile firing was to turn his key in the missile arming panel. That took only ten seconds to accomplish, but Vortmet always made the political officer remain on station for the entire drill, which took hours.

"I also want to conduct extensive passive sonar sweeps at all times," he continued. "Change operators as often as you wish, but keep them sharp. I do not wish to have any American submarines detect this launch."

Somolov nodded. The Americans had an annoying habit of trailing Soviet missile subs, hanging back in the baffles, the sonar blind spot directly behind the missile boat. On two of their cruises, a Los Angeles–class attack submarine had pursued the *Omsk* for days, breaking off only when Vortmet had gone to combat status.

On this mission, they had cleared their baffles frequently and at varying intervals to detect any pursuers. So far, none had been detected.

"Captain," Somolov said hesitantly, "I am nervous about this launch." Vortmet sat watching his second in command, his face devoid of expression. "I mean, we have never fired a nuclear missile before."

"There is no difference, my friend," Vortmet answered, "we do not set the policy nor pick the response." He handed

Somolov his cup to refill. "We are merely the sword, not the arm, nor the mind."

Somolov refilled the captain's cup and left to begin the drills.

"I want a big turnout for the public execution!" Mowati stressed, warming to his favorite hobby. "Have the radio and television make the announcement." He stood and cupped his chin in his hand, his index finger tapping the side of his wide nose.

"We will use the scaffold that is already in place," he went on, "I do not wish to waste time constructing another." He grinned wolfishly. "Besides, the last pair executed there were traitors. How fitting that the next two are saboteurs!"

Fido ignored the saboteur reference. Mowati had concocted the story to explain the capture and execution of two foreigners plucked from the sea. He had recommended to Mowati that they quietly dispose of the two men after they wrung the last bit of information from them, but Mowati could not resist the opportunity for a bloodthirsty spectacle. The two men would be killed the next day at noon. Fire would again be the method of execution.

"What is being done now about the missiles?" Mowati asked, breaking into Fido's musing.

"Captain Patno from your submarine *19th of January* will be going down with the diving bell tomorrow morning, Excellency," Fido replied. "They will determine how to bring up the atomic weapons."

Mowati smiled and clapped his hands. The thought of possessing atomic weapons was thrilling him almost as much as the prospect of burning someone alive.

Outside, the sun was sinking below the horizon in another blaze of orange and pink. Fido smiled at the irony. So much brutality took place in a setting of such natural beauty. That was the way of nature, brutality cloaked in pretty colors.

Mowati continued to rant on about the atomic bombs and his own power, but Fido paid no attention. He would take the helicopter back out to the freighter after the execution. He wanted to hear Patno's reports firsthand, with no radio transmissions that could be overheard by snooping satellites. By nightfall, they would know what they would have to do to get the warheads out. After that, they could start taking them off.

21

"Cap'n Beecher," the voice on the intercom said, "we're picking up some radio traffic from Manawatu that you probably ought to hear!"

"On my way," Beecher answered, rolling off the narrow bunk.

Tanner met him in the passageway next to the radio shack, offering a steaming cup of coffee.

"Thanks, Milt," Beecher said as he stepped in behind the radio operator, "what you guys got for me?"

"We copied this off the air a few minutes ago," the petty officer explained. "It sounds like the folks we're supposed to be looking for."

He pressed the play button on the radio console's tape machine. The distorted voice called all the citizens of Manawatu to witness the execution of two foreign spies in the capital city the next day at noon.

"What do you think, Milt?" Beecher asked.

"Well, I suspect that crazy bastard has no shortage of folks to rub out as spies or traitors or whatever, but calling them foreigners makes me nervous."

"Me, too," Beecher agreed. "Call Sergeant Miller to the wardroom, Milt. I think his guys are going to get to attend this hanging party."

Minutes later, Miller tapped at the wardroom door, then stepped inside.

"Sit down, Sergeant," Beecher said. Miller took a seat across the table from Beecher. Although he had probably been asleep when summoned, he looked alert and was perfectly dressed, his black coveralls neatly pressed. Beecher realized that he did not remember the man's first name. He was always referred to as Sergeant Miller by the sub's crew and Top by his men. Beecher felt odd about not remembering Miller's name, and made a mental note to find out.

"Sergeant Miller," he began, "we received a radio broadcast from Manawatu a few minutes ago. The government of Manawatu invited the population to the execution of two foreigners tomorrow. We are afraid that the foreigners are the British captain and Mr. Moore from UnderSea Corporation." Miller nodded impassively.

"I want you and your men to be ready to attempt a rescue of those two men tomorrow, if necessary," Beecher said. "Can you do it?"

"Well, I don't know about *attempting* a rescue, sir," Miller drawled, "we don't usually attempt anything, we just do it. If you want us to snatch those two guys, we will be happy to do so."

Beecher smiled. "I knew I could count on you. Get to work on it and let me know when you have a plan worked out. If you need anything, just ask."

Miller stood, saluted, and disappeared out the door. Beecher pressed the intercom. "Bridge," he said, "find Mr. Jackson and send him to the wardroom."

Jackson was slower to arrive than Miller had been.

"Mr. Jackson, I have a request of you," Beecher asked, "can you locate the British submarine again and see whether your friends are on board?"

"Of course," Jackson answered, "that's what I had planned to do all along."

Beecher ran his fingers through his short, salt-and-pepper hair.

"We have picked up some radio broadcasts from Manawatu

inviting the public to the execution of two foreigners," Beecher explained. "We don't know if those two foreigners are your friend and that sub captain, but we aren't taking any chances." He looked at Jackson, whose face was now tight with concern.

"We want you to take your little sub to look for the *Revenge,*" Beecher continued. "If you can find them and take them off, great. If they are the ones the radio was talking about, we'll try to get them back the hard way."

"When do I leave?" Jackson asked.

"As soon as we get a little closer to the area," Beecher answered. "We're making flank speed now. You might want to get your sub ready to go."

"Thank you, Captain," Jackson said as he stood up to leave.

"For what?" Beecher asked.

Jackson smiled. "For not making me wait around to see what happens!"

Merganthal had only been asleep a few minutes when more racking coughs woke him again.

"How you doin', guy?" Moore asked, sitting up next to the bunk. Moore had been sleeping, or trying to, under the single cot.

"I think my guts are fried," Merganthal moaned, gasping for breath. "My lungs feel like they're on fire!" He sat up, coughed again, and spat a bloody mucus slug onto the cell's moldy floor.

Moore stood up on the bunk and looked out the window. The sky was still dark, but a thin line of gray was beginning to light the clouds on the eastern horizon.

"Think we'll get a last meal in here?" Moore wondered, sitting down on the cot.

Merganthal snorted. "Probably cut off our arm and feed it to us!"

Moore felt his own biceps. "Well, I was hoping for a nice

salad, but what the hell." He stood so Merganthal could lie down again.

"Got any idea how they go about it here?" Moore asked.

"These jumped-up little buggers usually like to do something flashy to impress the masses," Merganthal answered, "I just hope it's quick."

Moore stood and walked over to the bars, peering as far down the dank corridor as he could. There was no sound in the cell block at all. They seemed to be the only prisoners there.

The trial, if you could call it that, had been brief. Three men in uniforms of some sort had judged them, pausing only briefly to hear some fictional charges. The "prosecutor" had barely finished reading the charges when the court found them guilty and sentenced them to death the following day. That had been all there was to it. They had been gagged, blindfolded, and led from the courtroom to this dank cell.

Now they sat waiting for their executioner to come fetch them and carry out the sentence.

Moore forced himself to think about escape. The prospect was not likely, but even a slim chance was better than none. He leaned back on the bars, testing them. They were solidly embedded in the stone wall.

The window bars were just as solid. He grabbed one and put his feet on the wall, straining as hard as he could to loosen it from the wall. Nothing.

If they were to escape, it would have to be out the front door when their jailers came to get them. Considering Merganthal's condition, that seemed unlikely.

The *Sam Houston* had slowed to a crawl and come to periscope depth to get a satellite fix on its position before sending Jackson off on his rescue mission.

Two Navy SEALs would accompany Jackson in case he

needed help outside the minisub or firepower inside it. As he checked out the little sub's systems, Jackson watched one of the SEALs in the water outside unhooking the steel mooring chains that held it to the *Sam Houston*'s deck while the other loaded mixed-gas diving gear and two black nylon bags that Jackson assumed contained weapons of some sort into the cargo bay.

"You guys about ready?" Jackson asked as he finished his system check.

Morris, the taller of the two SEALs, came forward. "As soon as Rottman gets back in," he answered.

"Rottman is in," a voice said from the hatch. Pharmacist's Mate Rottman pulled his wiry frame into the sub and knelt by the hatch.

"Lock it up!" he said to someone standing below in the *Sam Houston.* Jackson heard the metallic thump of hatches being closed on both vessels.

Jackson slipped on his headphones and pressed the transmit button on his radio.

"*Sam Houston,* this is Rock Sucker," he said, "disengaging now."

Tanner's voice answered him. "Roger, Rock Sucker, good luck."

Jackson opened the valve that let water into the skirt. A moment later the little sub rocked free of its large host.

"Here we go," Jackson said to the two SEALs, who were both crouched behind him, looking out the Lexan bubble as the little sub sped toward the downed British vessel.

"You know," Morris said, "we'll get to the Brit sub about the time those guys are supposed to be executed."

"Thank you for sharing that," Jackson snapped, "I really don't need to think about that right now."

"Sorry," Morris apologized, "I just meant that if we could get there sooner and find those two guys alive, the rest of the team wouldn't have to crash the party on shore."

"I know," Jackson admitted, "I'm just really worried about my boss. He's a good man, and he's saved my butt before."

"We know the feeling," Rottman assured him. The two SEALs retired to the cargo bay and promptly went to sleep, using their weapons bags as pillows.

It was refreshing to be up on the freighter's deck after the oppressive confines of his damaged submarine. Patno inhaled deeply, savoring the salt air.

The sun was beginning to show on the horizon, a pale line under the clouds. The storm had moved off farther north and the sea was calmer than it had been in days.

The *19th of January* was on the surface a few hundred meters away, the two patrol boats keeping the towlines taut.

On deck, the freighter's crew was readying the bell for their descent.

Patno had spent the last hour searching his memories of his days on a British missile boat. He was confident that he could open the missile hatches, but retrieving the warheads was another matter.

That fool Mowati! he thought to himself. This is insanity! Does he think the British will just forget their submarine? Does he think the Americans will permit him to keep nuclear weapons?

"What a fool," he murmured under his breath, "has he forgotten Iraq?" Even if the British or the Americans did not take any action, the Soviets were sure to, he surmised.

The Soviets had sent that diesel boat to look for the British sub, too. He knew from his days with the Royal Navy that the Soviets were not a forgiving lot. They would find a way to punish Manawatu for sinking it.

Patno looked at his watch. There was still time for breakfast before he had to join that man Palatin in the bell. He turned toward the steps that led down to the galley.

"All right," Miller asked, "are we good to go?"

"Ouh rah!" the SEALs roared in affirmation. Each six-man team had their gear clustered around them, waiting for their turn in the two airlocks. Each team would lock out of the submarine and rise to the surface with their inflatable boat. On the surface, they would start the quiet motors that would power the boats to shore.

Once on shore, each team would move to their attack positions and wait for the signal to hit the Manawatuans and rescue the prisoners. From there, the plan was a bit vague, but the SEALs prided themselves on their ability to deal with changing situations.

"Alpha Team, Bravo Team, in the locks!" Miller called out. "Charlie and Delta Teams, stand by."

The *Sam Houston* had been a missile boat before being recommissioned as a special forces transport. Two of the missile tubes had been converted into airlocks for swimmers. Two other tubes had been replaced with storage bins for Swimmer Delivery Vehicles (SDVs). The SDVs were powered underwater sleds that could haul two divers and a load of equipment to submerged targets. They were not fast enough or spacious enough for this job, so the teams would be using their inflatable Zodiac boats to get to the beach in a hurry. The boats had room to bring the two prisoners back, as well.

The first two teams pushed their boat, now compressed into a tight tubular bundle, into the airlock and shoved it up above them, moving in under it with their weapons and personal equipment. When each team was ready, Miller shut the door to the airlock, gave the men inside a snappy salute, and turned the wheel that let the water into the lock.

In minutes the airlock was full of water and a red light

atop each lock came on to indicate that the outer hatch was open. When the teams were out of the airlocks, they shut the outer hatch behind them. Miller then pumped the water out of each lock so the next team could get in. The process was amazingly fast.

When the last team was on its way, Miller turned to Tanner, who was standing to one side, observing the lock-out, and pulled out a cigarette pack. He offered one to the exec, who shook his head.

"This is the part I hate," Miller said, lighting up one of the unfiltered Camels, "waiting." He looked up toward the outer hatches and Tanner saw on the man's face a look he had seen so often on Ward Beecher's. For both men, waiting was more painful than doing, the danger to themselves less important than the safety of those under their command.

"Come on," Miller suggested, "we may as well make ourselves comfortable. There won't be any news for a while."

The two left the airlock compartment, headed for the radio shack.

Lud Barksdale, team leader of Alpha Team, was the first man to pop to the surface, followed immediately by the other five members of his team. As the last of Alpha Team surfaced, Walter (The Wall) Prichard, leader to Bravo Team, followed.

In four minutes the twenty-four SEALs were all on the surface. Each group treaded water as their Zodiac boat inflated, rolling aboard as it stiffened. The first man on board each boat broke out the small silenced outboard engine and clamped it to the hard transom at the back of the Zodiac as the others scrambled aboard and opened the weapons cases.

Four members of each team were armed with silenced MP-5 submachine guns. One team member carried an M16 equipped with an M203 grenade launcher and the sixth man carried a shortened version of the M249 Squad Automatic

Weapon, a light, belt-fed machine gun.

In addition to the firearms, each team carried smoke, tear gas, and fragmentation grenades.

As the teams filled their combat vests with ammunition and pyrotechnics, the four Zodiac boats streaked toward the shoreline just beyond the horizon. Dawn was just lighting the sky as they spotted the deserted beach a mile from the old prison.

"Hey, Lud," Michael (Mick the Spic) Rodriques asked above the whine of the outboard, "what are we doin' with this Halon stuff again?"

"If you'd talk less and listen more," Barksdale answered, "you would've heard the S2 tell us that the psycho who runs Manawatu has a thing for burning people at the stake."

"Are you shitting me?" Rodriques asked incredulously.

Barksdale smiled. "You know I wouldn't shit you, Mick," he replied, "you're my favorite turd!"

Rodriques returned the smile. "Thanks, Lud," he said sweetly, giving the ritualized answer, "you're my favorite asshole!"

The other SEALs in the boat groaned at the old joke.

"At ease in the boat!" Barksdale snapped in mock insult. Ahead, the coastline of Manawatu appeared through the gloom.

"Lock and load, gentlemen," Barksdale ordered. There was a brief clacking of gun bolts, then the men in the boats became deadly silent.

The only sound was the splash of the water under the boats' upturned bows and the quiet hum of the engines as they pushed the four boats forward, leaving a thin phosphorescent line in their wake.

"It's about time, you slug!" Kinshat snarled as Billy Ballida walked up to the guard post. "I hope your sleep was not disturbed!"

"It was not my fault," Ballida protested, "the major had us piling wood under the scaffold." He unslung his heavy rifle and propped it against the low wall that ran the length of the beach on both sides of the narrow guard post.

Kinshat shouldered his rifle. As he stomped off, Ballida called after him.

"Don't expect to get any sleep!" he said. "You'll be stacking wood, too!" Kinshat made an obscene gesture as he walked off down the path toward the barracks.

Alone at his post, Ballida sat down on the wall, took the hard roll from his pocket, and gnawed at it. After a few bites, he yawned, stretching his arms up above his head. He was still in this position when the tall, black-clad man stood up from behind the wall, slipped his arm under Billy's chin, and broke his neck.

The beach slid up under the rubber boats as they coasted onto the sand. The boats were still moving when the men piled out of them and grabbed the rope handles, dragging the Zodiacs up the beach to the line of palm trees.

"Use the palm fronds," Barksdale hissed, "get 'em covered!" The men took the big fallen palm leaves and hastily covered the boats with them.

When the boats had been hidden, the teams moved out to their positions. The sun was coming up, so the men had little time to waste.

As Alpha Team moved along the low wall that ringed the prison, a disgusted voice caught their attention. Barksdale motioned the others to stop and silently crawled along the base of the wall. The speaker was berating another guard, whose tone indicated that he did not want to hear much from the first man.

After a brief exchange, the first man left and the newcomer settled into his routine.

Barksdale heard the man bite into something as he sat on the wall, his back directly above. Barksdale crouched, waiting for the sentry to offer him a target. The man yawned loudly, stretching his arms above him.

Barksdale stood, slipped his right arm around the man's neck as he brought his left arm up behind and hooked his right hand into his left elbow, locking the man's neck between his arms. He leaned forward into the man and then kicked his feet backward out behind him. Locked together, the two men fell to the sand behind the wall.

Barksdale heard the man's neck crack as they hit the sand. The sentry went limp, his spinal cord cut. Barksdale pulled the man down off the wall and pushed him against the wall as the rest of the team moved up beside him.

"Nice take down," Rodriques whispered, stripping the man's uniform off him. He turned to the others, holding up the coat.

"This fit anyone?" he whispered. Corporal Tony Caso took the coat and slipped it over his wet BDUs.

"I can wear it," he observed. He stripped off the black uniform and slipped into the dead guard's uniform. As he dressed the others quickly covered the guard's body with sand.

As soon as he was dressed Caso slipped over the wall and picked up the dead sentry's rifle, a very worn Belgian FN.

"Pretty quiet up here, boss," he reported, "no one between here and the main fence—wait a minute, we got company!"

"Ass breath!" Kinshat shouted as he walked back down to the sentry booth. "You were so late, you made me forget my blanket! Don't think I will leave it for you!"

Ballida was standing with his back turned, leaning on the wall, staring out at the sea.

"What is the matter with you?" Kinshat called. "Are you

deaf?" Ballida waved, but did not answer.

"Prick ooze!" Kinshat muttered as he reached into the sentry booth for the small blanket he carried when he drew night guard duty.

"I'll tell you one thing," Kinshat snapped, "the next time—"

Ballida turned and for a split second, Kinshat did not realize that he was looking at a stranger, not at his second cousin. Kinshat did not even see the black, thick-barreled gun in the stranger's hands, nor did he hear the two soft pops it made. The world went suddenly dark and Kinshat died before he even hit the ground.

"Christ, Caso," Rodriques complained, using Caso's wet fatigues to wipe the blood off the second sentry's shirt, "couldn't you make a bigger mess?"

"You're right, Mick," Caso answered from the other side of the wall, "I shoulda got him hooked on heroin so he coulda OD'ed for us real neatlike."

"Fuck you," Rodriques replied, struggling into the wet khaki coat. Caso looked around and smiled.

"Don't tease me, sweet thing!"

"Both of you shut the fuck up and let's get on with it!"

"Roger that, Gunny," Rodriques answered, standing up and straightening the stolen uniform, "I'm ready."

"Let's hook it, then!" The team moved quickly up the path that led to the prison, the two phony Manawatuans leading the way.

"Wake up back there!" Jackson shouted.

"We're awake," a voice right behind him answered, scaring Jackson.

"Dammit!" he cursed as his skin crawled and a shudder ran through him. "Don't sneak up on me like that!" Morris chuckled.

"I thought you were asleep," the SEAL said, "you haven't moved for ten minutes."

"Why didn't you say something?" Jackson asked.

"Well," Morris replied, "either way, you were keeping us on course and up to speed."

Jackson shook his head. Maybe I was asleep, he thought, it's hard to tell sometimes when the water always looks the same and the motor's droning away in your ear. He checked the sparse instrument panel. They were still on course. They should be near the sunken sub in just a couple of hours. Above them, the surface of the sea was a bright emerald-green.

Behind him, he heard the two SEALs pulling out their equipment and checking their weapons, the click-clack of the bolts a too familiar sound to him.

Although he had been a submariner for years, when the round hatch in the bottom of the bell closed, Patno felt an immediate claustrophobia. Part of the problem, he realized, was that the bell was oriented up and down, unlike a submarine's horizontal orientation. The other problem he had was the bell's inherent helplessness. It could not rise on its own power or move without the aid of the crane above on the freighter. The powerlessness was terrifying.

Palatin, on the other hand, was happy to have a passenger who understood the underwater environment and who was not so heavily armed. Patno carried a pistol, but was clearly uncomfortable with it.

"We will enter through the hatch," Palatin explained, "I have the key!" He held up a T-shaped tool that looked more like a tire iron than a key.

"It turns the lugs inside," he demonstrated. "We will have no trouble getting into the submarine."

Patno nodded, his thoughts on both the sunken British

submarine and his own wounded sub.

But for God's grace, he reflected, his submarine could be lying on the bottom, its crew, himself included, drowned or crushed to death.

His morbid musings were cut short by Palatin's excited cry.

"There!" he shouted, pointing ahead through the gloom. He took the microphone and began giving instructions to the crane operator. In minutes they were hovering over the hatch, which seemed to reach up to meet them. The bell settled onto the British sub with a pronounced thump that made Patno's breath catch in his throat. Palatin went to work on the hand pump in the bottom of the bell and after several minutes of frantic pumping, he cracked the bell's hatch. Below them, the missile boat's hatch gleamed.

Palatin dropped down on it, inserted the large key, and turned it. The hatch opened beneath him and the two men dropped down into the now deserted British sub.

To Patno there was an eerie equality to the submarine. It was so silent and empty, unlike the crowded, busy place it should be. Aside from the eerie stillness, there was a disturbing familiarity to the British sub.

Although the *Revenge* was not like his old *Orpheus*, it still had many of the same English features, giving it a distinct déjà vu.

"Is it not incredible?" Palatin asked. He seemed to feel that the British sub was his alone, that he had discovered it like an archaeologist opening an ancient tomb.

"It is an amazing boat," Patno agreed as the two men made their way down the passageway to the command center. Palatin immediately started down the ladder to the missile room.

"We can begin immediately to open up the missiles," Palatin said enthusiastically. Patno stopped him.

"Do not be in such a hurry, my friend," he cautioned, "we are not in a race against time, but against failure. We will take our time and make sure we know what we are doing."

And I will take my time to visit this wonderful boat, he admitted to himself. As Palatin came back up into the room, Patno began a slow circuit of the room, studying the equipment and layout of the missile sub's command center.

Compared to his own boat, it was spacious and almost otherworldly. The equipment was dazzling and complex. A thrill of envy ran through him, followed immediately by a sense of relief that he did not have to command such power in the service of a lunatic like Mowati. He noticed a half-empty pack of Player cigarettes on the navigator's table and pocketed it.

After touring the command center, the two men went down the ladder toward the missile room. They passed through the galley, which had been so recently used for a hospital. Although there were bloody bandages and other evidence of injuries, there were no bodies. The absence of any crew in a boat that was not flooded was even more disturbing.

"The crew," he asked Palatin, "what happened to them?"

"They were rescued by a commercial vessel of some sort," Palatin answered, "I do not know the details, but the two we collected were waiting for the others to return."

"Then we are under a deadline," Patno muttered. The rescue vessel would certainly come back with some armed escort. He decided to cut short his nostalgic visit.

"Come, my friend," Patno advised, "let's get to work."

The door to the missile room was jammed and the wheel that retracted the locking lugs would not budge.

"I will get the welding torch!" Palatin blurted, turning and running back toward the bell. Patno, filled with misgiving, sat down and leaned against the stubborn door, lighting up one of the purloined cigarettes.

"This submarine will be our undoing," he muttered, patting the cold steel deck, "we should leave it in peace."

Patno was snubbing out the cigarette when Palatin came back down the ladder, noisily dragging the welding kit.

Rodriques and Caso peered around the gateway, looking through the iron gate at the scaffold in the center of the plaza. A crowd was gathering in the bleachers nearby, spectators who had come early to get a good seat for the execution.

"Looks like they're gearing up for a bonfire in there," Caso observed. "There's a lot of logs under that scaffold."

"What a nice guy!" Larry Talbot, the M249 gunner, commented.

"A real progressive," Barksdale added. "Any sign of the prisoners?"

"Not yet," Rodriques answered. He pulled the cover off his watch dial. "We still got half an hour before the main event."

Barksdale held the microphone of his small radio up to his mouth. "Bravo, Charlie, Delta," he whispered, "status?" He held the small headphone against his ear, listening.

"The others are set," Barksdale said, "as soon as we see the prisoners, we go." The four others nodded their assent.

"Prisoners!" Fashel Jendy shouted. "I am ordered by the holy court to bring you forth this day for execution of your sentences of death. Make peace with Allah in preparation for meeting him!"

"Fuck you, very much!" Moore answered. He stood up, reaching down to help Merganthal to his feet. The British captain seemed dazed, his eyes rolled around as he fought to get his bearings.

Four jailers brushed past Jendy and grabbed the two prisoners, binding their arms in front of them with rough cord.

One of them led Moore out of the cell. The others dragged Merganthal along. The corridor led to a door through which bright sunlight shone.

Outside, Moore was surprised to see a lawn tractor with a cart behind it waiting for them.

The jailers tossed them into the cart and tied their hands to the front rail.

"Good-bye, fools!" Jendy laughed as the tractor coughed to life and lurched off toward the prison's main gate.

"What do you see?" Barksdale asked as the sound of a loud sputtering motor echoed off the prison's stone walls.

"Un-fuckin'-believable," Caso observed. "There's two tied-up white guys." He stepped back and let Barksdale move up, handing him the binoculars.

"A riding mower?" Barksdale asked rhetorically. "This is too surreal for me!"

"Let's make it real!" Talbot suggested.

"A-ffirmative," Barksdale replied, pulling his mike close. "Bravo, Charlie, Delta," he whispered into the mike, "go on my signal."

Moore looked up at the blackened metal scaffold. The smell of diesel fuel wafted by, coming off the large pile of wood under the scaffold.

"Looks like we're fucked puppies, Titus," he said, "I hoped they would just shoot us!" Merganthal was looking at the people crowding into the bleachers.

"Not enough of a show, I suppose," he speculated as the cart pulled up to the metal stairs that led up to the scaffold's platform.

"Silence!" one of the executioners standing at the base of the stairs barked. He backhanded Merganthal as another untied Moore's hands from the rail. Moore pitched sideways and swung both hands, hitting the man under his jaw. The executioner, not expecting such behavior, was caught off guard and knocked back against the wood stacked under the scaffold.

The crowd cheered. Executions were more fun if the condemned fought until the last. This one promised to be very entertaining. A blow to the back of his neck brought stars to Moore's eyes. The man who had untied him had slammed a fist into him to bring him back into line. Others pulled him and Merganthal from the cart and dragged them up the stairs.

On the platform, Moore could see two rings in the platform's floor. Above them, two blackened steel cables dangled from the crossbar overhead.

Moore's hope sank as the men dragged them over to the cables and looped the steel strands around their wrists. As others on the ground pulled the cables taut, the men wired their feet to the rings in the floor.

As the executioners finished their work, a figure in a brilliant white uniform, wearing a chestful of ribbons and a plumed pith helmet, mounted the steps and walked up to the platform.

The gaudily garbed figure walked over to the two prisoners, his hands clasped behind his back, as if he were reviewing troops.

He said nothing, but stood looking at them proudly.

"What are you looking at, Dicknose?" Moore growled.

The smile vanished from the popinjay's face. He turned and walked to the front of the platform.

"Citizens of the Republic," he shouted to the crowd, "today you will see the price of spying against the people of Manawatu!" He turned and waved his arm at the two men strung up on the cables.

"These foreign agents have tried to kill your leaders and

destroy the Republic!" he went on. "What would you have me do?"

The crowd roared a chorus of "Kill them!" and "Death!" as the little martinet beamed.

"Death it is!" he answered, holding both hands up over his head. He turned to the prisoners.

"Thank you so much for your wonderful gifts," he hissed. He smiled another feral smile and walked off the platform.

Below on the ground, Moore could see the executioners lighting torches. Prefering not to watch them, Moore concentrated on the crowd. They were laughing and cheering, waiting for the main event. Off to one side, two of Mowati's soldiers were sauntering up to get a closer look.

The smell of burning diesel fuel stung his nostrils as a wisp of black smoke drifted by.

"This feels better, Malachi!" Mowati exclaimed, clapping Fido on the back. The dictator was beaming. The weather was fine, the crowd was excited, and the nuclear weapons were within his grasp!

Next to him, Malachi Fido was watching the fire leap to life under the scaffold. His face showed no emotion, but then it never did.

Below, in the bleachers, the crowd was jeering festively at the two condemned men. A few meters from the bleachers, two soldiers stood watching the show.

The two soldiers had black bags slung over their shoulders. Mowati watched as the two soldiers unzipped the bags and reached inside.

"Malachi," Mowati asked, following Fido's gaze, "who are those soldiers? What do they have in those bags?"

Fido squinted at the pair below and watched as they withdrew two black gas masks and slipped them on. Fido did not stay long enough to see the men take the gas grenades from the bags and throw them into both the bottom and the top of the bleachers.

The crowd, intent on the spectacle on the platform, did not see the gas grenades until they popped, spewing a dense cloud of pale smoke. A second later the tear gas seared their noses, throats, and eyes. The crowd surged into motion, screaming and pushing as they fought to escape the burning vapor.

As the crowd panicked, the two soldiers pulled two red cylinders half a meter long from their bags. They pulled pins from the ends of the cylinders and tossed them into the fire under the scaffold.

The staccato rattle of automatic weapons burst above the crowd noise. The wooden roof of the reviewing stand splintered as bullets slammed into it above Mowati's head.

The fire under the two prisoners suddenly went out, smoking furiously. The two men in the black masks then ran to the metal frame and quickly climbed up on the scaffold. Once on the platform, they ran to the two men.

As Mowati watched openmouthed, one of the two men aimed his weapon, a short black gun, at the crossbar above the prisoners. He fired a burst at it. The cable holding up the British captain flew apart and the other man pulled the Englishman down flat on the platform. As he did so, the shooter fired at the cable above the American, severing it as well.

Explosions rocked the reviewing stand. Puffs of black smoke drifted by. Mowati threw himself onto the floor as the wood overhead splintered again.

He looked for Fido, but the man was already gone, disappearing like he always did.

Mowati rolled over and pulled the chrome Walther pistol from the patent leather holster on his hip. He could not remember whether the little pistol was loaded. He pulled back the slide and it locked open. The magazine was empty. More explosions boomed outside and screams followed the booms. Mowati crawled toward the door, hoping to get out of the reviewing stand alive.

"Wait!" Caso advised Rodriques as the flames began to spread under the scaffold. The crowd was cheering and Caso wanted to use that distraction to cover their opening remarks. When the flames began to lick up through the metal platform, Caso snapped, "Let's do it!" Both men reached into the bags and pulled out their M17 masks, slipping them on and clearing them. With their masks in place, they reached in the bags and pulled out the four CS gas grenades, pulling the pins and letting the spoons fly.

Rodriques threw his grenades high up in the bleachers as Caso tossed his underhand beneath the front row. It took a second for the gas to hit the crowd, but when it did, all hell broke loose in the bleachers.

Beyond the bleachers, Charlie and Delta Teams, the fire support teams, opened up on the prison's guard towers and the individual guards on the grounds.

Bravo Team opened up on the reviewing stand, raking it with M249 and M16 fire and with grenades from the M203 launcher on the M16.

Using the panic in the stands and the suppressive fire to cover them, Caso and Rodriques pulled the red Halon extinguishers from their bags and tossed them into the fire. The Halon vapor quickly replaced the oxygen in the fire, snuffing it out.

With the fire under control, the two men climbed the scaffold's metal frame. As they mounted the platform, Caso pointed at the British captain, who hung limply from the cable. Caso caught the man around the waist and held him as Rodriques fired a short burst at the cable, cutting the wire.

As Caso lowered the British captain to the platform, Rodriques shot away the cable holding the American.

With the two prisoners on the platform, Caso and Rodriques untwisted the wire holding the prisoners' feet.

"Mr. Moore, Captain Merganthal," Caso shouted above the din, "we're Navy SEALs, we're here to rescue you!"

The American prisoner began to laugh. "You crazy bastards," he yelled, "I'm damn sure glad to see you!"

"Can you run?" Caso asked.

"Fuckin'-A, I can," the American answered, "just get me on my feet!"

Caso rolled off the back of the platform and reached up as Rodriques lowered the British officer onto his shoulder. Rodriques then dropped to the ground and helped the other prisoner off the platform.

"Go, babe!" Rodriques shouted. As Caso ran for the gate, lumbering along with Merganthal on his shoulder, Rodriques covered them from the platform.

"Got another gun for me?" Moore asked.

Rodriques shook his head. "Not here," he answered, "we'll get you one, though!"

As Caso neared the gate, Rodriques motioned Moore forward.

"Come on," he shouted, "let's go!" The two men dashed for the gate as a fusillade blasted around them.

By the time they reached the gate, Moore was coughing loudly, tears running down his face from the tear gas and smoke. Merganthal was out cold.

"We're out of here, Bark!" Rodriques shouted as he and Moore burst through the gate. The three black-clad men pulled gray smoke grenades from their BDU pockets and tossed them into the prison compound.

As the smoke billowed, Barksdale spoke into the tiny microphone on his headset, then pulled a flat, black H&K

flare gun from his breast pocket and fired three red flares into the air over the prison.

The SEALs threw more tear gas into the cloud of smoke and ran for the beach.

The Zodiacs were just as they had left them. Caso and Rodriques stayed behind at the guard booth to watch for any pursuers while the other four uncovered the four boats. Talbot shouldered the now unconscious submarine captain and carried him to the beach.

"Talbot," Barksdale snapped, "swap me!" He handed his submachine gun over and took Talbot's belt-fed SAW and the bulky plastic two-hundred-round reload magazine. "Take Moore and the captain here and get them on the way out."

Moore helped the two other SEALs pull the Zodiac down to the water and held the rubber boat in the gentle surf as Talbot lowered the injured captain onto the boat's wooded floor.

With Merganthal safely loaded, the others piled into the boat. Talbot started the outboard and the boat sped away toward the waiting *Sam Houston*.

"Bravo, Charlie, Delta," Barksdale hissed into his microphone, "where are you?"

"On the way, Alpha," the other teams answered. A minute later Bravo Team burst through the brush along the road and dashed down to the palms where Barksdale waited. Minutes later the other two teams appeared. Behind them, shots rang out.

"We got company!" Rex Cobble, Delta Team's leader, snapped as he dropped to the sand and whirled around. "A squad of bad guys got on to us just as we pulled out. We popped a couple, but the rest are still coming."

"Bravo, Charlie," Barksdale ordered, "hit the water! Delta, you stay with me!" He leaned up and shouted to the two ersatz Manawatuan soldiers in the guard booth.

"Caso, Rodriques," he yelled, "over here!" The two khaki-clad SEALs rolled over the wall and clambered down the beach to Barksdale's side.

As Bravo and Charlie Teams hauled their boats down to the water, the others formed a ragged perimeter to face the pursuing Manawatuans. They were not long in coming.

From the direction of the prison, the sound of a straining diesel engine and grinding gears drowned out the two small outboards.

"Theey'ree heeeree!" Rodriques whined. Around the bend in the road half a mile away, a six-wheeled armored car swung into view, the small turret atop the car swiveling toward them. Orange fire flashed from the turret and slugs whined overhead, sending up geysers of water as the gunner opened up on the boats in the water. Before Barksdale could give the order, the other SEALs on the beach opened up on the car with the SAWs and the M203 grenade launchers.

The gunner in the armored car swung his gun around as the 5.56mm slugs ricocheted off the car's steel hull, searching for the source of the fire.

One of the 40mm grenades hit the car's right front tire, breaking the axle. The tire twisted sideways, slewing the armored car to a stop.

"Pour it on 'em!" Barksdale shouted as the car's rear door opened and soldiers spilled out onto the road, firing wildly as they ran for cover in the trees. Two of the running men spun to the earth as bursts of fire from the M249s walked across them. The others dove behind the palm trees, firing frantically at their unseen attackers.

"Cap'n Beecher," Tanner called, "it's Barksdale! They're on their way back, coming in hot!"

"Bring the sail awash," Beecher ordered, downing his coffee, "sharpshooters and Stinger to the bridge." He ran for the command center. There, Tanner was waiting, standing under the hatch that led up into the tall sail.

"Sail awash!" the helmsman called. Tanner cracked the hatch and stood back as water splashed down. Beecher was first up through the hatch, his uniform soaked by the seawater. Behind him, the two SEAL snipers shouldered their way onto the bridge, their scoped M14 rifles seeking targets on the shore. Behind them, another SEAL with a long green Stinger missile launcher crowded up into the bridge.

"Snipers!" Beecher said, pointing to the vehicle turned sideways in the road. The two riflemen searched the shore with their telescopes for a second, then began firing at the flashes in the trees next to the stalled armored car.

"Mr. Tanner," Beecher bawled into the intercom, "what have we got in the tubes?"

After a brief pause, Tanner answered, "Two Mark 48s, one Harpoon, and one SLAM."

"Fire the SLAM, bearing one-eight-five, range twelve hundred," Beecher ordered.

"Sir, the SLAM won't have much time to get a picture on!" Tanner replied.

"It doesn't matter!" Beecher shouted. "Shoot it anyway!"

"Roger!" Tanner answered. "On the way!" Several seconds passed as the snipers continued to fire at their targets far away.

Beecher watched the water in front of the *Sam Houston*, waiting for the Standoff Land Attack Missile canister to surface. The long blue canister suddenly popped up to the surface nearly a hundred meters away. In a flash of fire and smoke, the top popped off the canister and the fifteen-foot-long modified Harpoon missile shot into the sky on a long tongue of flame, curving toward the bearing set in its guidance computer. The rocket booster cut off just as the infrared sensor picked up the armored car's hot exhausts. As the missile's sustainer motor cut in, it pitched sharply down, streaking into the trees just behind the car. The five-hundred-pound high-explosive warhead detonated just above the ground, engulfing the armored car in flames and shredding the palms with fire and hot steel.

Behind them a loud roar caught Barksdale's attention. He looked over his shoulder to see a missile streaking up from the water. Beyond the missile, partially obscured by the launch smoke, the *Sam Houston*'s sail jutted up out of the blue water.

"Yeah!" Barksdale shouted. "Let's *go*!" His voice was drowned out by the thundering crash from the trees behind the armored car. The concussion from the blast shook the palm trees above them, showering them with palm fronds as they pulled at the remaining Zodiac.

Barksdale and the two machine gunners kept up a constant fire as the others dragged the remaining boat into the water and started the engine, rolling into the boat to give cover fire to the men still left on the beach.

"Go! Go!" Barksdale shouted as the SEALs in the boats opened up.

The two machine gunners grabbed up their guns and sprinted for the waiting boat. Barksdale came up the rear, pumping bursts into the silent tree line. As Barksdale splashed into the boat, Caso gunned the motor. The Zodiac sped toward the dark sail.

For several minutes after the missile blast, there was no return fire from the Manawatuans, but finally, the machine gun in the car's turret stuttered to life. A line of splashes cut across the water and stitched the fleeing Zodiac.

Barksdale howled as a slug tore through his calf and others

ripped holes in the side of the boat. Roland Thompson, the M203 grenadier, fired again at the armored car. He had three 40mm rounds in the air before the first slow-moving grenade landed in front of the car. The second grenade went off on top of the car and the third hit the car's armored front. The turret gun again fell silent.

Barksdale's boat, punctured by the lucky burst, began to collapse.

"I hate it when this happens!" he complained, pulling a combat dressing from the pouch on his web belt as water began to pour over the rubber gunwale.

"Good shooting, Mr. Tanner!" Beecher complimented the executive officer as the tower of black smoke rose over the trees. The two SEAL snipers had put their rifles aside to help the men in the rubber boat. The British captain was unconscious and had to be hauled up the ladder like a feed sack. The other SEALs and the civilian with them scrambled up the ladder with alacrity.

As the last SEAL scrambled up into the bridge, he unslung the submachine gun from his back and emptied the magazine into the Zodiac boat, which promptly sank.

Between the sub and the beach, two boats were skimming over the swells, their little motors leaving thin white wakes.

Through his binoculars, Beecher saw the last boat leave the beach, motoring flat out for the safety of the sub. It was several hundred meters from the beach when the gun in the armored car opened up again. Beecher watched in horror as the burst stitched across the Zodiac.

The teams in the two nearer boats had seen Barksdale's boat get hit. One of them spun around, returning to pick up the men in the damaged boat. All of the SEALs but the man at the motor rolled out of the boat into the water, making room for the men he would have to pick up. The other Zodiac picked up the men in the water and continued on toward the *Sam Houston*.

"Who is that going back?" Beecher asked the SEALs already on board.

"Looks like Prichard, sir," they answered.

"Relax, boss," Rodriques urged, pointing across the water at the boat racing back to pick them up, "help is on the way!" Their riddled boat was almost full of water now, just the tops of the two undamaged cells keeping it afloat.

"I'm a Navy SEAL," Prichard shouted as he spun his boat around and pulled alongside, "I'm here to rescue you!"

"Oh, fuck you!" Barksdale growled as he rolled out of his own sinking boat into Prichard's. Caso, Rodriques, and Thompson followed Barksdale. As Prichard gunned the motor, Rodriques riddled the sinking boat, which quickly disappeared beneath the bright water.

Ahead, the other boat, heavily laden with the men from Prichard's boat, bumped against the submarine's sail. The SEALs scrambled up the iron rungs, disappearing down into the sub, the last man shooting up the Zodiac before dropping down after the others.

The water ahead began to jump as bullets from shore again sought them. Barksdale looked back at the beach. There was now a truck next to the armored car and troops were piling out of it.

Some crouched near the truck, firing as the others ran down the beach, shooting from the hip at the fleeing boat.

On the sub, the snipers were back at work, keeping the enemy on the beach busy as the last of the Zodiacs pulled alongside the *Sam Houston*.

Barksdale was the first one off the boat, hopping on his good leg up the ladder with the others following.

Prichard, the last man aboard the Zodiac, reached up for the iron rungs on the *Sam Houston*'s sail, swung his stubby gun around, and shot up the boat before climbing up after the others.

As the last SEAL climbed down the ladder into the command center, Beecher shouted to the crew below.

"Dive, dive!" he shouted, following the others into the submarine as the blue Pacific rose up the sides of the sail.

Inside, the SEALs were running down the passageway toward the troop bay, clearing the area for the sub's crew to work.

"Hard left rudder!" Beecher shouted. "All ahead flank! Let's go get that little sub and then get the hell out of Dodge!" He turned to his exec.

"Mr. Tanner, take the con," he said, calm returning to his voice, "I'm going to see to our new guests."

The *Sam Houston* rolled slightly to port as the nuclear sub dove into its turn.

In the sick bay, Sgt. Miller was joking with the wounded Barksdale.

"As you were," Beecher said as Miller stood. He looked at Barksdale's leg. There was a neat hole on the inside of his calf and a three-inch rip on the outside. Barksdale was smiling, but Beecher could tell the smile was forced.

"We got 'em back, sir!" Barksdale crowed.

"Looks like you paid a price for them, Sergeant," Beecher observed.

"Lucky hit!" Barksdale demurred. "I thought that SLAM had taken care of them."

Beyond Barksdale, Dr. Channing, the ship's surgeon, was bending over the unconscious Brit. The civilian hovered nearby.

"How is he, Doctor?" Beecher asked.

"Mr. Moore here says he got worked over pretty good, Captain," Channing replied, "all the jostling didn't help, but he seems stable now."

Beecher turned to the civilian. "You Moore?" he asked.

"Moore or less." The man chuckled wearily, extending his hand. "Thanks for coming after us."

"You have a friend who wouldn't hear different."

"Where is Tom?" Moore asked.

"He's looking for you back at that captain's missile boat," Beecher replied. "We're on the way there after him now."

The fear on Moore's face mirrored his own as he turned from the sick bay and returned to the command center.

22

Eli Kandar's head hung down onto his chest. He had gotten only minutes of sleep in the last two days. The strain of battle and the terror they had all felt when the *19th of January* had been hit had exhausted him. The active sonar was off and Kandar was using the CSU 3-4 passive array to monitor the activity in the area. There had been no contact of any sort since they had found the British submarine below.

He longed to get some real sleep, but with the captain gone, Lt. Askart was keeping the boat at battle stations.

Dozing, he missed the faint whirring sound that swept under the *19th of January*'s hull.

Both the SEALs were crowded up against his back, looking up at the dark shapes above on the surface.

"Shit!" Morris whispered. "The whole fuckin' fleet must be up there!"

Rottman was more taciturn. "Their whole fleet is a couple of PT boats and maybe one submarine," he drawled. "We'll be in and out before they know we're here!"

"I hope you're right," Jackson whispered. Overhead, a large dark shape loomed on the surface.

Jackson slowed the little sub. Ahead, two dark lines led from the surface down toward the bottom.

"Looks like they got here first," Jackson observed. He tilted the joystick forward, following the dark lines down.

As the gloom deepened, Jackson switched on the sub's lights, pointing them down toward the sunken missile boat.

Illuminated by the lights, the dark lines became a thick steel cable and a thicker rubber hose. The hose and cable led them down to the *Revenge.* Perched atop the dark hull was a bright blue spherical bell.

"What the hell is that thing?" Jackson asked.

"I'll be damned!" Morris answered. "An old diving bell!"

Rottman shoved his head over Jackson's shoulder. "This doesn't look good for your boss," he observed, "I'll bet they're not there now."

"Maybe not," Jackson said, his voice flat and angry, "but I can keep these fuckers here for a while."

He maneuvered over to the cable and hose and shut down the thrusters. Gripping the control stick that moved the little sub's manipulator arm, Jackson extended the arm and caught the steel cable, closing the clawlike hand around it.

"Now," he said, "this is for Bob Moore." He twisted the knob atop the control stick. A thick blade dug into the cable, but stopped. Jackson worked the manipulator hand back and forth, trying without success to sever the cable.

"Shit," he muttered, "it's too tough." He opened the claw and reached out to snag the thick hose. The cutter blade sliced easily through it.

"There," Jackson said, "at least they'll have to hold their breath!" He went back to sawing on the cable.

Rottman interrupted him. "Before you get too carried away," he suggested, "why don't we see if we can hear anything going on in there?"

"How?" Jackson asked, pausing to look at the two SEALs.

"We've got an acoustic tap with us," Morris answered. "We can listen in to the folks in there with it."

Jackson turned back to his control stick. The manipulator hand sprang open, releasing the cable. He turned the thrusters up and pushed the sub down onto the deck next to the diving bell.

Again the pumps cleared the water between the two vessels, sealing the smaller sub to the larger one. Rottman and Morris were hovering over the hatch, a small nylon bag between them. At Jackson's signal, they popped the hatch and Morris dropped silently down onto the *Revenge*'s hull. Rottman handed him a cone-shaped device on the end of a long wire. As Morris placed the cone on the hull, Rottman pulled a pair of headphones from the bag and slipped them on. He reached into the bag, fiddling with something in it, then smiled and nodded at Morris, who climbed back up into the little sub.

"Whaddaya got?" Jackson asked from the pilot's seat.

Rottman held up his hand, concentrating on the headphones.

"There's a couple of guys in there," he reported. "They heard us set down and they found out you cut the air hose." He smiled. "They're pissed!"

"What was that?" Patno asked. Palatin, concentrating on cutting through the missile room door with his torch, stopped and looked up. He had been cutting on the door for nearly an hour now, cutting one lug at a time, trying to make the small acetylene bottle last.

Patno motioned for him to cut the torch. It popped softly as he turned the knob that shut off the flammable gas.

"What?" he asked, tugging the dark green goggles off.

"I heard something," Patno answered. Palatin, suddenly concerned, stood.

"Inside the sub?"

"No," Patno shook his head, "outside, I think, on the hull."

Both men heard a muffled thump above them. The two

men looked at each other, then raced back to the upper deck to the bell.

The deck under the open hatch was wet and water was dripping from the hatch into a large puddle beneath.

"No!" Palatin shouted. He ran under the hatch and looked up, searching for the source of the leak.

"What is it?" Patno asked. Palatin shook his head.

"I do not know," he answered, "there is no leak around the skirt." He climbed up into the bell. Patno stood underneath, watching as Palatin ran his hand around the bell, searching for wet spots.

"Oh, no," he moaned, looking down at Patno, "the air hose has been cut!"

"How can you tell?" Patno asked.

Palatin ran his hand around the circular filter under the hose fitting. Water ran off his hand. "The valve shut when the line was cut," he explained, "a little water got through before the valve closed."

Palatin jumped down and shut the missile sub's hatch.

"Are we stranded here?" Patno asked. Palatin shook his head.

"No," he replied, "not unless the cable is cut, too." Palatin looked up as if trying to see beyond the steel hull.

"Who could have done this?" he snapped, his voice rising. "What fool managed to cut the hose?" He began to pace under the hatch, looking up.

"I will cut the balls off the idiot who did this!" he shouted. "The minister will skin him alive and make boots with his worthless hide!"

Patno leaned against the bulkhead as Palatin ranted on.

"Do you hear Bob Moore or the British captain?" Jackson asked. Rottman shook his head.

"No, I only hear the two of them," he replied, "I don't

hear anything else in there at all." He looked up at Jackson. "I don't think your boss is in there"—he shrugged—"I'm afraid that's who's going to get it today on shore."

Jackson glanced at his watch. It was 1:30 P.M. Whatever was happening on shore had already begun. He flooded the skirt and pulled free, turning the shuttle sub to the compass heading that would reunite them with the *Sam Houston.*

Wilson Roosevelt stuck his head out of the sonar room and shouted at the group in the control room.

"Shut the fuck up!" he insisted. "I can't hear a fucking thing with you mothers smoking and joking in my ear!" The loud knot of SEALs broke up and Roosevelt went back to his scope.

Thin lines danced hesitantly across the cathode tube. He closed his eyes, straining to hear any sound on the hydrophones. He listened for a moment, then watched the scope as the lines suddenly blazed into sharp relief on the screen. He pressed the intercom switch to the command center.

"Sonar contact!" Roosevelt called. "Maximum range. Sounds like surface ships."

Tanner's voice came back on the speaker. "On the way," he replied. A minute later the *Sam Houston*'s executive officer stuck his head into the cramped sonar room.

"Whatcha got, Roosevelt?" Tanner asked.

"I think we found that Limey sub, sir," Roosevelt answered. "If we did, there's a party goin' on right over it."

"Keep on 'em, Wilson," Tanner instructed. "We're going to slip up on those guys, if we can. Let me know when you have a better fix on 'em."

"Will do, sir."

"Sonar has the surface group over the sub, sir," Tanner reported, "he's sorting them now."

"Did you reload the empty tube?" Beecher asked.

"No, sir," Tanner answered, "it's still dry."

"Load a Harpoon in it," Beecher instructed him. "Pull the Mark 48s and load Harpoons in them, too. We're going to give those little rats a taste of high tech."

As Tanner turned to the weapons station, Beecher thumbed the intercom. "Sick bay," he said, "have Mr. Moore come to the wardroom."

Beecher was pouring another cup of coffee when Moore tapped on the door and stuck his head in.

"You wanted to see me?"

"Yes, Mr. Moore," Beecher replied, "want a cup?"

Moore nodded and took the offered cup of steaming brew. "Call me Bob," he said, sitting at the narrow table. Beecher sat across from him.

"Your friend was tortured?" he asked.

"Captain Merganthal," Moore answered, "yeah, those monkeys put him through the mill."

"They were after his missiles?" Beecher asked.

"Just the warheads, I think," Moore said, "they didn't seem to be interested in the missiles themselves."

Beecher was silent for a moment. "We can't let them get those reentry vehicles, you know."

Moore smiled. "I wouldn't worry too much about that," Moore stressed, "Merganthal left them a little surprise." Moore's eyes suddenly got wide. "Jesus Christ!" he exclaimed, standing so quickly he bumped the table and spilled the coffee from his cup. "We've got to get Tom out of there! Those missiles are booby-trapped!"

"What?" Beecher asked, dodging the hot coffee that ran off the table.

"Merganthal wired the hatches!" Moore blared. "If they open any of the missile tubes, one of the warheads will blow!"

"Holy shit!" Beecher exclaimed. He pressed the button on the intercom panel. "Con, this is the captain," he said, "get those tubes loaded now." He turned toward the door, the coffee forgotten.

"Come with me, Mr. Moore," he requested, "we have a lot of work to do."

23

"I got 'em, Skipper!" Roosevelt called. Beecher and Tanner both stood outside the sonar room as Roosevelt punched up the data on his display.

"Got 'em on the BQR-21," Roosevelt explained. "There's one big target, probably a support ship or a freighter, three smaller ones that sound like patrol boats, and something else that I can't quite make out that's not making any power noise at all."

"Five altogether," Beecher observed. "Well, we'll take on the ones that can hit back first and go for the other two later." He turned to Tanner. "Ready all tubes for firing!"

"Get me a tight lock on those suckers, Rosey," Beecher demanded, "I want to hit 'em all the first time!"

"Will do, Skipper!" Roosevelt answered, returning to his scopes.

"After the Harpoons launch," he told Tanner, "load One and Two with Harpoons again and put Mark 48s in Three and Four. I want to get off a second round as quick as we can."

"Will do, sir," Tanner assured him. Beecher turned to Moore. "I don't know where your friend is, yet," he told him, "but we'll make sure those scum on the surface don't get him."

"If they haven't got him already," Moore added. Beecher said nothing. Moore had voiced Beecher's own fear.

Roosevelt's voice interrupted his silence.

"I got 'em locked, sir," he called, "DIMUS is tracking now! Targets at five-zero miles."

The DIMUS (Digital Multi-Beam Steering) would track five targets simultaneously.

"Feed it into the Harpoons," Beecher directed.

Moments later Roosevelt called, "Locked in, Skipper!"

Beecher turned to Tanner, who was waiting for his order.

"Fire One through Four," Beecher ordered. A slight shudder ran through the sub as the four missile canisters were ejected at five-second intervals from the *Sam Houston*'s torpedo tubes. The UGM-84A Harpoons would skim the surface of the water, searching for the targets assigned them by the fire-control computer.

Tanner ticked off the missiles as they launched. As each canister left its torpedo tube, the torpedo room crew shut the tube's outer door, pumped it dry, and reloaded it with either another Harpoon missile or a Mark 48 torpedo. The Harpoons could strike targets as far away as 118 miles. The Mark 48s could hit targets over twenty-three miles away.

"Go to emergency speed, Mr. Tanner," Beecher ordered, "red-line the reactor."

"Emergency speed, aye," Tanner answered. "Full power on the reactor."

"The best we can make is twenty-two knots," Beecher told Moore. "We'll try to find your friend. I have two of my people on his sub, too."

Moore nodded. "I've been on one of these sub transports before, Captain," he told Beecher, "I used to be a SEAL myself."

Beecher looked at Moore and grinned. "I should have known," he said, "you guys always turn up in the damnedest places!"

• • •

Eli Kandar yawned and stretched, trying to work the kinks out of his back.

When, O God, he wondered, when will we be allowed to sleep again like men? The sea was heavier now, and the *19th of January* was rolling side to side now. Kandar ignored the slight nausea that the rolling was causing, concentrating on how stiff his back was and how numb was his backside.

He was in midstretch again when he heard the far-off *ka-bong* of an underwater sonar.

His blood ran cold. The *19th of January* was a sitting duck now. They could fire their two torpedoes, but without the power to maneuver, they could not avoid a hit.

A cold hand closed over his heart as he turned to Askart, who was slumped in a chair, staring at the wall.

"Sonar contact, sir," he said sadly, "sounds like a submarine's active sonar."

Askart sat staring at him for a second as his report sunk in, then Askart blanched. "What?" he stammered.

"I have a sonar contact!" Kandar snapped. "Active pinging! Another submarine!"

Askart jumped to his feet, his eyes wild. He dashed to the radio.

Kandar sought to isolate the sound and determine its source and direction as Askart warned the little fleet of the danger.

Chostsa was speaking to the captain of the freighter when his radar operator shouted. "Captain Chostsa," he called, "I have something on my screen."

"What is it?" Chostsa asked, telling Whitcox to wait a moment.

"I don't know," the operator said, "it seems to come and go."

"How far is it?"

"About twelve miles away," the man estimated.

"When it comes back up, let me know." Chostsa returned to the radio. "Do you have anything on your radar?" he asked the *Star of Islam*'s captain.

Whitcox went off the line to check his radar screen. "Nothing," he answered, coming back on the air.

"Let me know if you pick anything up—" Askart's voice on the radio cut across his transmission.

"Alert!" the submarine officer shouted. "Submarine alert!"

"Submarines?" Chostsa asked. "Where? How far?"

There was no answer. "Dammit, Askart," Chostsa demanded, "where are they and how far?"

This questioning was cut short by a thunderous blast that shook the patrol boat's cabin.

Chostsa whirled, staring out the side window as one of the patrol boats towing the submarine disappeared in a cloud of black-tinged orange flames.

"What the hell!" he exclaimed. His cry was cut short by a second explosion that engulfed the other patrol boat, cutting it in half and blowing the superstructure up into the air.

Behind the two destroyed patrol boats, the damaged submarine wallowed in the swells as debris rained down on it. As Chostsa watched, a white blur streaked over the two burning boats and spiked down onto the submarine, striking it just in front of the sail. The *19th of January* disappeared in a cloud of black smoke and orange flames.

When the smoke cleared in a few seconds, Chostsa could see that the submarine had split in two. Only the round bow and the twisted, broken propellor showed above the water.

Chostsa tore his eyes from the destruction and whirled toward the helmsman, who stood openmouthed at the boat's wheel.

"Emergency speed!" Chostsa screamed. "Hard right rudder!"

The man stood frozen for a second, then rammed the throttles up, spinning the wheel as the patrol boat shot forward.

Chostsa grabbed for a handhold as the boat pivoted. He turned back to watch the sky off the port side. He was staring at the horizon when the white missile slammed into his boat from above. The deck jumped from the impact, then blast and flames swept through the bridge, incinerating Chostsa, the helmsman, and the other twenty-one members of Chostsa's crew.

"One hit!" Roosevelt called. "Two hit!" He pressed the phones to his ears. On the scope, another wide band flashed across the screen. "Three hit!" Roosevelt reported. A wide grin spread across his dark face. "Four hit!" he shouted. "A clean sweep, sir!"

"Excellent!" Beecher enthused. He picked up the intercom microphone. "This is the captain," he said to the whole crew, "all four of our Harpoons have scored hits. My compliments on your outstanding shooting." Muffled cheers rang out from the deck below.

"Cap'n," Roosevelt called, straining to hear above the noisy crew, "Cap'n! I hear something else!" Roosevelt punched the faint sound into his computer, which quickly spat back a printout.

"It's that little sub, sir!" he shouted. "That Jackson guy!"

"Get a fix on him, Rosey," Beecher replied. He turned to Moore, smiling.

"Looks like we'll get everybody back this trip."

Panic reigned on the *Star of Islam*'s deck. Half the crew were clutching the rail, staring at the burning remains of the three patrol boats. The submarine had disappeared completely. Only an oily spot of floating debris marked the spot where it had gone down.

There had been no more missiles, for which Whitcox was very grateful. The *Star of Islam*, tethered to the sunken submarine below, was an easy target.

Unarmed, it could not defend itself in any way from the submarine that the *19th of January*'s sonar operator had detected moments before the missiles struck.

Whitcox was now on the line, trying to raise the pair in the British sub.

"What should we do?" Palatin asked. Since Whitcox had called them about the attack, Palatin had been terribly frightened. When Whitcox suggested that they come back up, Palatin had been eager to do so.

"We will certainly be sent back to get the warheads," Patno assumed. "We should make it easy on ourselves. We will open all the missile tube hatches so that we can simply set down on each one with the bell and extract the weapons."

"Fine," Palatin agreed, "let's do that and then go to the surface as fast as we can. I am scared to death down here!"

"We will be all right, my friend," Patno assured him, "trust me." The two men closed the missile sub's hatch and went back down to the missile room.

Inside the long, dark missile room, Patno stood before the missile launch panel and read aloud the instructions that Minister Fido had radioed out to them earlier.

"First, switch the panel to Test Mode," he read. He turned the round switch, lining up the arrow on it with the word TEST. The panel lights all shifted to test status.

"Switch each outer hatch door to OPEN," he read on. Patno moved down to the panel where the twin rows of missile status lights glowed red. He reached down to the first switch under a plate that read TUBE 1. The switch was labeled HATCH STATUS. He turned the switch to the setting marked OPEN.

"Here we go!" he said casually.

24

Jackson struggled to keep himself calm as the *Sam Houston*'s long black hull slid beneath them. Behind him, Morris and Rottman hooted and high-fived each other.

The red hatch glowed under the lights and Jackson steered over it, bumping along the hull until they came to rest over it.

"Everybody out!" Jackson called, rolling up and out of the front bubble as the two SEALs popped the hatch. The *Sam Houston*'s hatch opened beneath them and the two SEALs dropped down into the sub.

Jackson followed, stiff from his long stint in the small pilot's chair. Sitting on the edge of the hatch, Jackson was relieved to see Bob Moore's face looking up.

Jackson pushed off and dropped into the sub, falling into a pile on the wet deck at Bob Moore's feet. Moore helped him up and the two men hugged, clapping each other on the back.

"Man, I thought you were a goner!" Jackson exclaimed.

"You were damn near right!" Moore answered. He pointed to the SEALs standing nearby. "If these guys hadn't shown up, we'd have been crispy critters by now!"

"I hate to interrupt your reunion, gentlemen," Lt. Tanner broke in, "but we need to get the—"

The collision alarm blared, drowning out the conversation.

"What the?" Tanner mouthed. He pushed through the crowd, reaching up for the strap that pulled the hatch shut. As he got a grip on the strap, the *Sam Houston* moved as if it were being pushed sideways by some huge unseen hand. A loud, dull boom rang through the hull.

A solid column of water poured through the hatch, slamming onto the deck and sweeping those in the passageway off their feet.

Tanner, his hand through the hatch strap, slipped and twisted, disappearing in the column of water. Moore and Jackson were knocked down and pushed along the deck by the roaring water. Moore struggled to his feet, only to be knocked down again. The lights went out, plunging the sub's interior into darkness for a second until the dim red emergency lights came on.

As abruptly as the water had come, it stopped. Tanner, both hands now clutching the hatch strap, hung from the closed hatch.

"Gimme a hand here!" he sputtered. Moore and one of the SEALs slogged through the water to the dangling officer. Moore pulled on the strap as the SEAL reached up and spun the locking wheel. The SEAL slipped again as the submarine surged forward. Moore held on to Tanner, scrambling to get a footing on the wet deck.

"Oh, God!" Moore wailed. "The stupid bastards did it!" The speaker overhead interrupted.

"Damage reports!" Beecher's voice squawked. "Lt. Tanner, report!"

Tanner untwisted his wrist from the strap and pressed the intercom switch a few feet down the passageway.

"Tanner here," he answered, "some flooding under the emergency hatch. The hatch is closed, repeat closed. No casualties." He looked at Moore. "I think we lost the civilian sub," he added. Tanner started forward to the command center with Moore following. Jackson scrambled to his feet and followed the two men, splashing through the water that still clung to the deck.

Beecher was waiting for them. "Well, Mr. Moore," he said, his irritation evident in his voice, "your friend's booby trap worked pretty well." Alarm horns were honking and damage control reports were pouring in from the sub's different sections.

"How bad is it, Captain?" Tanner asked.

"Could be worse," Beecher observed, "the reactor's okay and we still have full power. We've got a few leaks, but we can handle them."

"What are you going to do now?" Moore asked.

Beecher stared at him. "We're going to run like a bunny, Mr. Moore," he stated flatly, "we're going to run like hell!"

"What do you mean they got away?" Mowati yelled into the phone. "Got away to where? This is an island! Find them!" He slammed down the receiver.

"I will not permit this insult!" he shouted, cowering the crowd in his spacious office. "They will pay with their lives!" He pushed away the doctor who was dabbing at the scratch on his arm. A splinter from the reviewing stand's riddled roof had cut his skin, but the idea of the attack itself had cut him worse. Now his pride was at stake.

The group of courtiers and hangers-on in his office knew that if he could not punish those who had perpetrated the attack, he would punish those who had allowed it to happen or even those who happened to be standing nearby when his rage finally peaked. No one wanted to be the scapegoat.

The attack had done little actual damage. Half a dozen soldiers had been killed in the plaza, two had been found near the sea wall, their uniforms stolen.

Most of the casualties had come on the beach when the submarine-launched missile blast had killed a dozen troops and damaged an armored car.

Mowati refused to believe the story about the submarine, claiming that submarines fired torpedoes, not missiles. There was alleged to be wreckage from the attackers' inflatable boats, but Mowati refused to look at it, saying he wanted to see dead men, not wet junk.

"Where is that Malachi Fido when I want him?" Mowati asked. No one knew. No one ever knew where Malachi Fido was.

Mowati slumped in his chair, exhausted from the fear he had suffered during the attack and the frustration he was forced to endure now. His arm was starting to throb again.

"Get all our airplanes in the air," he bellowed. "Have them search for them!" As an afterthought, he added, "If there is a submarine, have them find it."

The military men in the room all bowed out, happy to get away from the stormy ruler.

"I figure we were about twenty klicks from the blast," Tanner answered. "We're lucky the Brits have smaller warheads on their MIRVs."

"And lucky the *Revenge* was down in a trench," Moore offered, "that focused the blast."

"We were close enough, thank you," Beecher said. "When that Brit wakes up, we'll tell him he doesn't have to worry about anyone getting his sub."

The intercom speaker squawked. "Cap'n Beecher," Roosevelt's voice crackled over the box, "you'd better come listen to this!"

Beecher stood and left the wardroom with the others following in his wake.

In the sonar room, Roosevelt was waiting. "It sounds like a seismic tremor, sir," he explained, handing Beecher a set of headphones. Beecher listened, then passed the phones to Tanner.

"It started a few minutes after the bomb went off," Roosevelt went on, "and it just got a lot louder!"

"What do you think?" Beecher asked.

Moore interrupted. "I suspect the bomb set off that fault line it was sitting on," he speculated. "That's probably a tsunami building up now."

"It would appear that my poor boat will get to strike back from the grave!" a voice said from behind them. They all turned. Titus Merganthal stood leaning on the attack periscope, a wan smile on his face. "She took the bastards with her," he said, then collapsed.

25

The droning engines caught his attention over the droning voices in the room. Mowati looked out the window. Overhead, the two Pucara planes soared toward the ocean north of the island. Below, the Army was deploying all its battalions along the wide white beach, protecting the president from the threat that had already passed.

Tomorrow, his generals and that fool of a prison warden would pay for their failures!

Mowati was planning the exact nature of those payments when the boom rattled the windowpanes. Everyone turned toward the windows. Outside, there was nothing to see as far as the horizon.

"Can you see it?" the pilot asked, his voice rising in pitch.

"No," Mowati's aide answered into the radio, "we can see nothing yet."

"It's moving fast!" the pilot stressed. The Pucara's pilot claimed that the sea was rising around the blast site, producing a huge wave.

Mowati stood at the window, brooding.

The wave was no problem, he knew, it would just dissipate long before it got here. The problem was the warheads. There could be no doubt what had happened. His fool of a submarine commander had managed to set off one of the

British warheads and destroyed any hopes for a Manawatuan nuclear force.

First I am denied the pleasure of cooking those two spies, he fumed, and now I am denied my atomic bombs! Everyone connected with this disaster will pay, even Malachi Fido.

Where is that snake? Mowati wondered. Outside, the horizon seemed to slowly rise up in the sky, hanging there as it deepened in color to a dark blue.

Lost in his thoughts of revenge, Mowati did not notice it until the others in the room began shouting and running out the door.

Mowati stood riveted as the tall wall of water bore down on Manawatu. It picked up the boats and ships in its path, flipping them like toys in a bathtub, then swept over the beach, thundering up the side of the hill until it blotted out the sky.

Mowati was standing in his window, staring openmouthed at the towering sea, when it slammed into his palace and swept it, along with most of Manawatu, into the South Pacific.

They had watched the disaster from the air. The wave had completely inundated the islands for several minutes. The higher elevations had finally emerged from the foaming water, but most traces of habitation were gone.

"What do we do now, Minister?" the pilot choked.

"Fly a course three-fifty degrees," Fido suggested, "and look for a place to land!"

As the pilot banked the plane around, Fido looked down at the ruined islands. There would be survivors, of course. In a few weeks, he would come back to look for another puppet leader.

26

"Comrade Captain," Somolov called through the door, "Pacific Fleet is on the VHF and they're hopping mad!"

How can they know when I am asleep? Vortmet wondered as he sat up on the bunk and pulled on his trousers. It never fails.

In the corridor, Somolov was waiting for him.

"We received a signal on the ELF ordering us to make contact," he briefed the captain as they made their way down through the ship, "I sent up the VHF buoy."

In the communications room, the radio operator held a headphone out to him. "The line is secure, Comrade Captain," he said as Vortmet slipped the phones over his head.

"Go ahead, Pacific Fleet," Vortmet said. He was stunned when Fleet Admiral Ganilev's voice boomed in the headphones.

"Vortmet, you idiot," Ganilev thundered, "what have you done?"

"I have done nothing, Comrade Fleet Admiral!" Vortmet answered.

"You received no order to fire on Manawatu!" Ganilev roared. Vortmet reached up and turned down the volume to his headphone.

"That is correct, Comrade Fleet Admiral," he agreed, "we have not fired on anyone. We are on the bottom, waiting for orders."

There was a long pause. Finally, Ganilev came back on, his voice much subdued.

"Return the *Omsk* to base," he ordered, "and, Captain, all your missile launchers had better be full." The line went dead.

"What was that all about?" Somolov asked. Vortmet shook his head.

"You remember what I said about the arm and the sword?" he asked.

"Yes?"

"Well," Vortmet said, "I'm not sure why, but I think the arm is about to shove the sword up our butts."

27

"But—" LeFlore tried to interrupt.

"But nothing, Marc," McLaughlin snapped. "They rescued a whole submarine full of British sailors right under that tin horn dictator's nose!" The Old Man walked around the desk and sat on the edge of the polished ebony desktop.

"Who cares about a piddling cargo sub?" he went on. "We'll write it off, for God's sake!"

"But, Mr. McLaughlin," LeFlore protested, "everywhere the man goes, trouble follows him! Bob Moore is a one-man disaster area!"

McLaughlin looked out the window, an odd dreamy look on his face.

"Marc," he said, "the world is a dangerous place and the ocean is unforgiving of even the slightest mistake." He looked at LeFlore with a stare that made him squirm. "Bob Moore's job is to go in harm's way for UnderSea Corporation!" LeFlore started to reply, but McLaughlin held up his hand to silence him.

"He's the one man I'd like to have with me in a disaster, Marc," McLaughlin asserted, "and I want to do something for that wounded SEAL, what's-his-name?"

"Barksdale," LeFlore answered.

It was no use. The Old Man had bought into Moore's bullshit again. LeFlore stammered through his usual lame brownnosing and backed out of McLaughlin's office.

Elgin Bickerstaff, Moore's shaved gorilla, was waiting in the president's outer office.

"Great news about Bob, huh?" he smirked. As LeFlore passed, Paula, McLaughlin's secretary, picked up the phone.

"You can go in now, Mr. Bickerstaff," she said, giving LeFlore a look of supreme condescension.

"Later, Marc!" Bickerstaff called as LeFlore shut the president's door behind him.

"Later, your ugly ass!" LeFlore muttered. He wandered back down to his office, searching for some way to shit in Bob Moore's mess kit.

SWAMPMASTER

They crawled up from the radioactive garbage of America's second Revolution. The armed enemies of freedom, they swarm across occupied Florida like a fungus. The enslaved masses fear them. The lucky few escape them. One man defies them . . .

His name is John Firecloud. A Native American trained by an ancient shaman in the ways of survival—and armed with a graphite compound bow—he leads a fight-or-die quest for blood and honor in a post-nuke America gone straight to hell. The swamps are his battlefield. His mission is freedom. His methods, extreme . . .

Turn the page for a sample
of this exciting new series,

Firecloud pressed a finger to the protective medicine pouch of *aha lvbvkca* and cedar leaves hung from his neck, and uttered a silent prayer to gods he scarcely believed in anymore.

He ran the fingers of his other hand down the smooth, curved fiberglass and graphite limb of the compound bow slung over his shoulder. Eight steel-tipped broadhead arrows nosed out of the snap-on quiver.

Their lethal sting was something in which he had *absolute* faith.

His decision made, Firecloud climbed off his perch and went scrambling down the tree trunk. This time he didn't need the fluttery murmur of the leaves to conceal the sound of his movement. The descending copter made racket enough.

His feet quietly touched ground moments before the acne-scarred man reached the trees.

The trooper stood whistling before a tall red mangrove whose twining prop roots snaked aggressively toward the sandbelt. He had not been in a good mood, but a sense of imminent relief had improved it—that and simply being off the beach. He hadn't really thought anyone would be scoping him if he took a leak down there; at least not anyone who mattered. The thing was, he hadn't wanted to watch the copter land. Because watching it land made him think about having to board it in just a few minutes.

And when he so much as thought about boarding it, his stomach rolled as if it were already struggling with gravity.

If he'd told Vic that, Vic might have gotten the impression that he was some kind of wimp. Which was far from the case, as the Indian woman could attest. He had showed her just what kind of man he was when they'd broken into the clapboard shack she had been living in. Yeah, he'd gotten her underneath him and showed her, and it had been fine.

A justifiable hatred—not a fear, oh no; if anyone ever suggested it was some kind of irrational fear, he would beat that person to a pulp—of flying did not make him a coward. Man, he believed, had not been meant to fly. Birds flew. Goddamned bugs flew, which was why they had been given wings. Human beings did not have wings. Because they were not meant to fly. Simple logic.

He loosened his Sam Browne belt, unzipped, and began extricating himself from his pants.

He never finished.

Without warning, a hand shot out from behind and clamped over his mouth, its thumb and forefinger pinching shut his nostrils. Simultaneously another hand came around and gripped his throat. He was pulled backward, off balance. He tried to breathe, tried to scream, could do neither. His air was cut off, he was choking. His feet flailed, heels skidding on the mushy ground. He brought his own hands up and pried frantically at the arms wrapped around him. His nails bit into them but they wouldn't unlock. Their muscles bulged. The powerful fingers gripping his throat tightened. His Adam's apple was being crushed. His windpipe was swelling shut. Blood rose into his mouth, filled it, rose into his nose. The pressure in his head was enormous. He was drowning, drowning in his own blood. A haze fell over his vision. Red at first, then shot with black. Then the haze became a solid wall of black.

Just before the end he made a desperate attempt to beg for his life but could only manage a tiny, sputtering sound.

Then he went limp.

John Firecloud let the body spill out of his arms.

Blood spouted from its nostrils and gaping mouth as it crumpled into a mesh of prop roots.

Firecloud looked at the soldier and noticed the spreading wet stain on the crotch of his half-fallen pants. Death had robbed him of whatever dignity he'd possessed . . . just as he'd robbed it from the woman.

Still doesn't make them even, Firecloud thought.

He turned and watched through the trees as the Strikehawk banked for a landing. It hovered about ten feet above the ground for several moments, the wash of its rotors whipping up a funnel of sand, then settled gently onto its landing gear.

The men on the beach approached the chopper cautiously while its slowing blades beat lazy circles in the air, their captive trailing along behind.

Firecloud nocked an arrow into his bow and waited. The helicopter had come down with its starboard side to him, which meant he would be out of the pilot and co-pilot's direct line of sight. A lucky break. Now if he could only have another . . .

Upper and lower doors opened on the Strikehawk's fuselage like a square, robotic mouth.

His breath catching, Firecloud anxiously peered inside.

And got his second break.

The cabin was vacant; even the big 7.62 sidegun was unmanned. One of the men in the cockpit must have opened the doors remotely.

Firecloud exhaled with a grateful sigh. He had counted on the Strikehawk having a reduced crew since cabin space was needed to accommodate the ground patrol and their captive. But even a third of its maximum troop complement would have been sufficient to make him a vastly outnumbered goner. That there was no one aboard besides the flight crew was a discovery which exceeded his best hopes. Possibly the absence of any effective threat to their occupation had resulted in a slackening of the Front's military procedures.

The odds were still four-to-one against Firecloud, but he felt that he at least had a fighting chance.

He readied the bow for firing, testing its draw.

Watching. Waiting.

Inertia had finally brought the Strikehawk's blades to a halt. The aircrew had popped their windscreen canopy and the co-pilot was outside the front of the craft having a cigarette. The man named Vic and the other foot soldier had lead the Seminole woman aboard, after which Vic had emerged from the copter alone, walked slowly over to the co-pilot, and grubbed a smoke off him.

The two of them talked and puffed while in the cockpit the pilot undid his safety harness and relaxed with his helmet visor up, stretching his arms, occasionally joining in on the conversation.

Several minutes later the co-pilot stubbed his cigarette into the sand and gazed over at the trees. He said something to Vic, who turned in the same direction.

"Ray, you done yet?" he shouted, taking a last drag off his cigarette and flicking away the butt.

His only response was silence.

Firecloud added a little more tension to the bowstring.

Vic looked at the co-pilot and wagged his head, a prosy grin on his face. "Guy's bladder must hold more water than

Lake Michigan," he remarked. He cupped his hands over his mouth and looked back at the trees. "Yo, Ray! You playing with yourself in there or what? We gotta take off before the bad weather hits!"

There was another parcel of silence broken only by the rhythmic slap of the waves and the cries of the gulls that had flocked inland before the advancing stormfront.

Vic's grin dwindled. "Bet he went and took a catnap, damned if he ain't sawing wood," he grumbled, shaking his head with greater annoyance. "I'll go and fetch him."

Firecloud heard more than a trace of the South in the tone and cadence of his voice. He wondered briefly if the man was a native of Florida; there were many collaborators, a percentage of whom had become full-blown National Front recruits.

Vic started quickly up the loose-packed sand toward the ridge less than thirty yards away.

Firecloud let him walk for ten yards, then took aim and fired.

An instant after the arrow whooshed from the bow he saw Vic stagger backward and look down at the shaft suddenly jutting from his chest, his face clenched with agony and utter bafflement.

He looked back at the trees with that same pain-wracked, stunned expression, opened his mouth as if to shout, and wheezed out a foam of blood and saliva.

His hands gripped the arrow and tried to pull it free, but only succeeded in further mauling the lung in which its tri-bladed head was imbedded. A scarlet flower bloomed in the center of his service blouse.

He gagged, pale pink blood bubbling over his lower lip and chin, and swayed forward.

Firecloud was off and running across the strand before Vic's face smacked the ground.

For a moment neither the pilot nor co-pilot could grasp what was happening. They stood watching with frozen, wide-eyed incomprehension as the man with the bow dashed toward them.

Then the co-pilot snapped back to awareness, looked desperately around for cover, and broke for the chopper's open passenger door.

Firecloud let him go. It was vital that he deal with the pilot next. If the man in the cockpit pulled down the armored canopy then he would be sealed off from attack.

As if reading Firecloud's thoughts, the pilot reached for the raised windscreen panel above his head.

He was a slice of an instant too late. Firecloud had halted less than fifteen feet from the chopper and loaded his bow. His firing hand a blur, he loosed the arrow, slipped another from the quiver on the bow's handgrip, and fired it in rapid succession.

Had the pilot's helmet visor been down, he might have lived a bit longer. But it wasn't, and he didn't.

The tip of the first arrow ripped into his exposed right cheek and plowed an exit wound through the left. Gaudy fletching protruded from a face that immediately stretched around the shaft like a distorted fun house mirror-image.

The second arrow drove home just as the pilot reflexively turned, gaping, toward his assailant. It socked into his right eye and burrowed deep into his head, throwing him spread-eagle backward across the cockpit.

His legs jerked twice then ceased to move.

Firecloud narrowly scrutinized the corpse for a moment, his lips compressed into a grim, tight line. He'd halved the odds against him. The Strikehawk was brain-dead.

A fighting chance, yes.

He raked his glance over his shoulder toward the cabin entrance.

And saw the surviving ground trooper jump from the boarding step and come tearing at him in a low, humpbacked charge, hands wrapped around an M-16. The co-pilot was in the sidegunner's station, calling to the soldier at the top of his voice.

"Come back, you idiot, I can't get a shot off with you in the way!" he shouted from the copter. "Goddamn it, I said *you're blocking my fire*!"

The soldier disregarded him. His eyes met Firecloud's with a steely, vengeful glare as, still running, he triggered a burst from the rifle.

Firecloud chucked his bow and dodged sideways just before a hail of lead riddled the ground on which he'd stood, churning up dry geysers of sand. The soldier swung his head around to see where he'd landed, pivoted toward him, triggered another volley. Firecloud managed to avoid the fire with a lightning quick tuck-and-roll.

"Gonna get you for Vic and Ray, bastard!" the soldier screamed, pivoting again to keep up with Firecloud's zig-zagging scramble. His berserk grimace revealed a mouthful of crooked, decayed teeth. "I'm gonna blow your guts right out your ass!"

The gun muzzle chattered, pulverizing a mound of ocean debris. Shell fragments and chunks of seaweed and driftwood sprayed chaotically into the air.

Firecloud ducked, bellyrolled, weaved. He was tiring, losing his wind. Every muscle groaned from exertion. He had to put an end to the barrage—*fast*.

Powering to a low crouch, he launched himself at the man with the gun, barely skirting a murderous stream of bullets. Caught off guard by his sudden move, the soldier tried desperately to recover from his surprise and draw a bead.

Like the Strikehawk's pilot, his reflexes were a hair too slow and that slowness cost him his life.

Moving with a speed and fluidity that was almost balletic, Firecloud came in under the M-16's barrel and then sprang to his full height, hooking the barrel between his left forearm and bicep. At the same time he slammed the heel of his right hand against the soldier's head at a point just above the nose and between his eyebrows, shattering his glabella.

The man died instantly as jags of bone ripped through his brain. He collapsed, his finger spasming on the gun trigger and squeezing a round harmlessly into the air.

Firecloud tore the M-16 from the soldier's convulsive grasp as he fell.

The rifle felt uncomfortable in his hands.

He did not like guns. Guns made killing easy and so depreciated life.

Did not like them, but knew how to use them.

He spun around, poised to fire the M-16 at the helicopter.

The chopper's sidegun was pointing back at him. The co-pilot held it steady with his right hand. His left hand was twisted in the Seminole woman's hair.

He pulled hard on a fistful of hair and she shrieked, bending backward into him, her spine arched against his shoulder.

Firecloud fixed him in a hard cold stare.

"Go ahead, Indian, do me," the co-pilot snarled. "But you'll be doing the bitch, too. That's if I don't put you down first."

Firecloud was silent.

"I'm not sure what's happening here, but if this is over the woman, you can have her," the man in the helicopter said. "Flying the chopper's my business. She isn't. All you've gotta do is toss the gun and I'll let her go."

Sure you will, Firecloud thought, still saying nothing. He was positive that the instant he relinquished his weapon he would be as dead as the soldiers sprawled about the beach . . . and the woman would be left at the co-pilot's mercy.

Neither his dark eyes nor his rifle wavered. He took a slow step forward.

Thunder rumbled over the Gulf.

"Stay where you are, man!" The co-pilot wrenched the woman's head back again and she cried out sharply, her cheeks blotching with hectic color. "I can hurt her if I want to," he yelled. Listened to the thunder. "I can hurt her bad!"

Firecloud kept his gun leveled. Letting each second live. Noticing every movement, as the shaman, Charlie Tiger, had once taught him.

Each movement means something, the old man had said. *Observe. Then participate.*

He took another step.

"Hold it!" the co-pilot screamed. "Is she gonna have to catch more punishment? *Is she?!"* He pulled her hair a third time. Tears burst from her eyes and she squirmed in his grasp, causing his weight to shift.

His hand slipped back from the trigger.

Just a little.

Just enough.

"No. No more," Firecloud muttered under his breath, firing the M-16.

It went off with a blinding roar, recoil slamming its stock against Firecloud's shoulder, empty casings leaping into the air around him. Thrown suddenly clear of the girl, the co-pilot dervished toward the far wall of the cabin, his head vanishing in a grisly eruption as a half dozen slugs plowed into it at once.

A shapeless, bloody pulp from the shoulders up, the co-pilot's body rebounded off the wall and toppled to the copter's steel floor with a dull clang.